THE BLACK WIDOW

THE BLACK WIDOW

John Newton Chance

Chivers Press · G.K. Hall & Co.
Bath, England   Thorndike, Maine USA

✓

70336

This Large Print edition is published by Chivers Press, England, and by G.K. Hall & Co., USA.

Published in 1997 in the U.K. by arrangement with Robert Hale Ltd.

Published in 1997 in the U.S. by arrangement with Robert Hale Ltd.

U.K. Hardcover ISBN 0–7451–8852–4 (Chivers Large Print)
U.K. Softcover   ISBN 0–7451–8886–9 (Camden Large Print)
U.S. Softcover   ISBN 0–7838–1996–X (Nightingale Collection Edition)

The text of this Large Print edition is unabridged.
Other aspects of the book may vary from the original edition.

Set in 16 pt. New Times Roman.

Printed in Great Britain on acid-free paper.

British Library Cataloguing in Publication Data available

Library of Congress Cataloging-in-Publication Data

Chance, John Newton.
  The black widow / by John Newton Chance.
    p.   cm.
  ISBN 0–7838–1996–X (lg. print : sc)
  1. Large type books.   I. Title.
[PR6005.H28B53   1997]
823′.912—dc21
                                                    96–42007

THE BLACK WIDOW

CHAPTER ONE

1

Mamsie Stong came out of the stone farmhouse and looked at the sky. It was blue, with small white clouds moving a little fast for the shiny yellow straw hat with blue ribbon she had bought for the Andrews wedding. She went back into the farm room and took up a blue silk scarf. She tied it over the crown of the hat and bowed it under her chin.

'I'll be out most today, Millie,' she called back through the kitchen door. 'I haves business to clear.'

'Right, missus,' Millie said, coming to the kitchen door with floury hands. She cocked her head in admiration. 'I do believe you're looking for another husband so soon.'

'No heart warms to a cold bed, Mill. Not that I haven't had the cold one long enough.' She went to the door again. 'Oh, and get Harry to slosh under the pump before he comes in the house. He slept with Queenie last night and she didn't farrow after all.'

'Sleeping with a pig! Needs his bloody head seen to.'

Mamsie went out, putting on her white gloves as she turned aside to the barn. She went in through the great doorway and looked for a moment at her Land-Rover, delivered an hour ago and looking as if it had been born a second time.

'Looks too pretty to go back to work,' Mamsie said, and went behind it to her bicycle which leaned against a roof post.

It was a bicycle she had had as a girl, twenty-five years before and given her by Aunt Jessie, who had bought it new twenty years before that. It had out-lasted Aunt Jessie.

Mamsie had cleaned it up yesterday and put oil in the gummed up little places just as she remembered doing all those years ago.

For today she was going back to start again. She wheeled out the bicycle right into the lane, then scooted it twice and hopped her right leg through the gap and dropped back on to the saddle. She wobbled. She swerved from side to side of the lane and fell off into the ditch. She got up, laughing, and brushed herself down with the white gloves.

'Tis good luck it's dry,' she said, and lifted the bike and mounted once more.

This time she pedalled away very fast so it was easier to keep balance. She pedalled as she had when a girl, when the basket on the front had been full of shopping and her yellow hair streamed out behind like a horse's tail, and behind her were the boys, two on two bikes, swerving in their efforts to catch up, and Jamey at the back bumping on a flat tyre; all trying to catch her.

That was when she used to swoop off the

lane, on to the farm and into the haybarn to let them catch her.

It was almost like really going back again. She even felt the same sort of devilment, but then, perhaps it had never gone; just been twisted a bit.

She had almost regained mastery of the cycling art when she came into the town, but the traffic was so surprised to see a bicycle like a hose rack being ridden so fast they gave her plenty of room.

She swooped into the stonemason's yard amid the tombstones, urns, surrounds, angels and cherubs and realised that she had not yet used the brakes. They made a frightful groan and scream noise but stopped her just in front of the wooden office and its impressive painted headboard reading, 'Tobias Harsden & Son, Undertakers, Stonemasons. All funeral Arrangements made. Also Plumbing.'

Tobias' grandson Jamey Harsden opened the office door angrily as he heard the noise, imagining some town boy was up to something. They had been up to quite a lot that morning. When he saw the big, pretty woman dismount unsteadily from the ancient machine he almost dropped his pipe.

'Mamsie! My dear! what *are* you doing?'

'I am starting again, Jamey,' she said, dusting herself down again, back and front.

As she bent to do it he had a fine view of that luscious bosom which had so moved him in the

3

past and still did, and still could later.

'My dear girl!' he said, going to her. 'You look beautiful! My dear—' he lowered his voice, '—but buried only yesterday, and you going about, looking only twenty and—I don't know.'

'You always did worry about what people would say,' she said. 'Adam's dead. And a bloody good job, too. If any man asked to be dead he did. You know none of the boys came back for the funeral. And that was proper. But they wrote to me. Dear boys! of course they wrote to Mum.

'David wrote he hoped I wasn't upset and would I like to go out and farm in Australia with him? Joe wrote he was sorry to hear it and he would come back and see I was all right, but he was thinking about marrying this girl in Durban and if he spent the money on the fare he would have to put it off, but I would understand because I always did.

'Sam was always the honest one, you know. He wrote he was happy for me and would write again to see when I felt like a holiday and he would arrange for all the tickets for me to go and have a holiday in Vancouver with him.

'Does it all worry you, Jamey?'

Jamey looked towards the yard gates as if uneasy about someone listening.

'People still get funny about the dead. You know that, Mamsie. As if any villain becomes a saint as soon as he's rotted off the vine. They

4

call this a permissive society, but what's new they permit I don't know. Seems to me the only change there's been is what we used to do naturally, they have to shout about it to get 'emselves in the mood.'

He began to laugh.

'That's better, Jamey,' she said, putting her arm through his. 'Now let's into the business room. Tis business I've come about, you know.'

Jamey felt a spasm of alarm that his bill for the funeral would not be met, but when he felt her arm in his, anxiety almost melted.

'Mrs Gawn is out,' he said, taking Mamsie through into the second room of the hut office. 'I have to have ugly ones that are married. That bloody woman insists.'

'Oh Jamey, that's naughty.' She laughed. 'Never mind. Tis about the epitaph to carve on the stone. I know you always do 'em yourself.'

'It's my trade,' he said. 'Some masons you get now have their own ideas about spelling which doesn't go down that well with the bereaved.'

'Well, here it is,' she said and put her hand down into her rich bosom while he watched.

'I remember you always kept things down there, Mamsie. And put them down there deliberate, too, and let us draw lots for who got it out.'

She laughed and he watched the bosom shake.

5

'Well, it was all a game, Jamey,' she said. 'We all enjoyed it, didn't we?'

'I wish I was back there to start again,' he said. 'But you went too far with that picking straws, Mamsie. It was the worst thing you ever did, that last time.'

'You needn't tell me, Jamey. But I thought it was fair at the time. I was all fluffed up inside with one asking and then all the others coming forward and saying they meant to—My God! I was a lucky girl up to then.' She looked out of the window, then shrugged. 'Still, that's over. At least, the cause of it's over.' She gave him the paper. 'The spelling is as I want it.'

He unfolded the paper then pulled his eyes off her and read what she had written. He looked up an instant, then read it again, his lips moving slightly as if making sure he had got it right the first time. Then he looked up.

'Mamsie!' he said between his teeth. 'I can't cut such words on a stone!'

'But it's my wish for him, Jamey. That's how I remember him and all about him and all boiled down like jam, and that's what it comes out as; short as can be made.'

She stood tall and firm, and he felt even greater desire from it.

'I can't do this, Mamsie,' he said. 'You know I'd do anything for you—ordinary.'

'My dear Jamey, any man would do anything for me—ordinary. This isn't ordinary. I'm not made a blessed widow every

6

day and I wish to remember twenty-five bloody years with that bastard in the way I want it!'

'I can't do it, Mamsie!'

'But it's not rude words. Nothing like that! It's just modern spelling!'

He looked at her, resolve melting, until he turned away in self defence and shook his head. 'I can't. It would cause a scandal!'

'He *was* a scandal!'

'Not like that. A scandal about you, Mamsie.'

'I tell you what, Jamey,' she said, taking another way round, 'I've got to see Eddy Worth about putting a notice in his paper, so I'll ask him and if he says it'll be all right, will you agree to that, then?'

Adroitly, he replied, 'Yes, you see Eddy, dear. That's a good idea. I've already—' he would have said, got name and dates on Adam's stone, but stopped.

'Already?' she prompted.

'I've forgotten what I was going to say.' He laughed a little ruefully. 'I always did forget what I meant to say when I was alone with you. How on earth I managed to say such things to that bloody woman I can't imagine now. I suppose that's how a rabbit gets himself caught. He goes around laughing at the snares and then gets fed up and says, "Oh bugger it! Here goes!" and there he is.'

'You mustn't think like that, Jamey.'

He folded the paper again and tapped it with

7

a finger.

'I'd like to cut this on stone to please myself,' he said, 'and I'd keep it where nobody else could see it. But I won't do anything that might hurt you, Mamsie. If Eddy says—' He shrugged.

She took the paper and would have spoken but the door suddenly opened and Nell Harsden came in.

'Oh, I'm sorry!' she said, looking surprised. 'I didn't know my husband was—'

'It's all right, Nell,' Mamsie said, smiling. 'It's settled now.'

'It's about the epitaph,' said Jamey with suitable solemnity.

'Of course.' Nell smiled like a mole trap.

'Mind if I leave my bike here?' Mamsie said, as she turned to go. 'I'll pick it up later.'

When she had gone out Nell went to the window and watched her going out of the yard, walking with long, easy paces.

'What on earth is going on?' said Nell. 'One day a widow and dressed up as if she's going to her second wedding! And a bicycle? What on earth's she doing on a bicycle?'

Jamey turned away. 'She's a woman,' he said.

Nell turned round at that.

'And what does that mean?' When she saw him shrug as meaning he didn't want to explain, she went on, 'What on earth will people think? One day a widow, next prancing about dressed as if she's going to her second wedding! And a bicycle? What on earth is she doing with a bicycle?'

'You have just said all that,' said Jamey. 'Or are you just talking to yourself out loud so that God can hear that you are still his chief agent?'

Nell turned from her last look out of the window at the bicycle. And she turned very slowly.

'Now that,' thought Jamey in sudden dread, 'has sown the seed of sheer bloody hell.'

Nell strode to the door and went to go out.

'What did you want?' said Jamey.

The answer was the slam of the door and the falling of Tobias Harsden in sepia from its place on the wall to a folded sack on the floor.

Nell often slammed the door.

2

The offices of the Post were quiet that morning. The paper had gone to press. The Editor, son of the Proprietor, who had retired from active life, was going through a few letters, drinking coffee and eating a biscuit at his desk. His room looked out on the town square over a window box thick with sweet peas.

His secretary came to the door open on to the outer office.

'Mrs Stong,' she said.

'Show her in Alice. Of course.' He tossed the letters into his basket, got up, looked into the gilt mirror over the fireplace inscribed

'Worthington's Pale Ale', then turned and went out into the outer office to meet his visitor.

When he saw her his surprise made him glance quickly over his seated staff as if to note any sudden reaction to the unexpected vision of the widow.

'My dear,' he said, as she smiled at him. He bowed his head slightly as she passed and went into the room. He followed, after flashing the Wash-Out look to Alice, banning further visitors.

He went in and closed the door.

'Mamsie, you look years younger,' he said, delighted. 'But you know it's usual to wear something a little prim for a few days.'

'I've been in mourning for twenty-five years, Eddy. This is the end and the beginning as the chap says on the tv.' She sat down opposite the Editorial chair and began to take off her gloves. 'I haven't got a bag because I came on a bike.'

He sat down, hands spread out on the desk and stared.

'On a bike?' he said. 'It's years since you've been on a bike. I don't think I could balance now.'

'I just learnt all over again,' she said. 'And as I haven't got a bag I have a few papers in between Silla and Carrybidis, as you called them, and a cheque book in my knickers, which was a mistake because it wouldn't bend with

10

the pedalling and when my knee came up it stuck in my tum.'

'Mamsie,' he said, grinning, 'but why go back to a bike?'

'Because I am starting all afresh in my personal relations and there are some things I want to know I can still do.' She put a hand down her dress and pulled out a piece of folded paper. 'Oh no, that's Jamey's—' she searched again, 'ah, here it is. That's yours. The Obituary.'

She put the paper firmly on the desk and held her hand on it and he put one of his on hers.

'You look beautiful, Mamsie. Why didn't you let me have the short straw?' He looked earnestly at her.

'Because I did it fair,' she said with big eyes. She eased her hand away.

He picked up the paper but stayed looking at her.

'It's not too late yet, Mamsie,' he said.

'Oh, come on you,' she said with a small laugh. 'You've had a fine old time as a bachelor, as I know. Why start thinking such things?'

'You know damn well I've thought about it a lot.'

'I think sweet peas are one of my favourites,' she said, looking at the window, and then back at him. 'I'm waiting to see what a literary man thinks about my epitaph.'

'I'm sorry, dear.'

11

He unfolded the sheet headed 'OCV Corn and Seed Merchants—Order Form', and read on below.

She watched his expression tighten, his eyes widen, his mouth twist up in one corner almost in alarm, and she thought; 'He was always the best-*looking* of them!'

He jerked his head up, his bright blue eyes still wide, shocked.

'Mamsie! I can't publish this!'

'But there's no rude words in it,' she said, with a touch of haughtiness.

'Rude words!' he said sitting back. 'Rude words might tone it down a bit—' Inspiration descended. He smiled and held out his hand. 'You are ever one for a joke, Mamsie. Where's the other? The one I've got to put in.'

She leant forward.

'That's the real one Eddy. That one you've got. That says what he was and what he did. And that's what I want him remembered by.'

Eddy changed his manner to consolation and sympathy.

'Mamsie, we all know what a time you had with him. It was a mistake at the start—'

'It was so, was it?' she said in sudden anger. 'Then let me tell you that he never thought so! He never thought there was anything wrong—for him. You didn't know that, I suppose? He was on a good horse. There was never a need for him to get off. If you've got a minute, I'd like to get a little off my chest that I kept quiet

12

about then and ever since.'

'I've got all day. You know that.' He thought to let her talk would ease her mind so she would take back the epitaph. And besides, for him, she could talk for a long time without him minding.

'As you know, I was eighteen when we wed. Nine months to the day I had my litter. Triplets! Nothing ever happened in small ways with him.' She laughed. 'And there was the first problem because three don't go into two without one yelling his head off and you feel cruel and that upsets the flow.

'Then Dolly Emery—you remember her? She used to help old Annie at the shop. Well she had one and more milk than she knew what to do with so she came down and we put two and two together and it went fine because it fed four and we worked it so nobody got upset.

'Well, of course she was there every day, and so was Adam, and he thanked her for her kindness very warmly, and the next thing we know a couple of the boys bring him back face down on a gate and moaning for the doctor.

'Then Dolly told me her husband shot him in the arse for chasing after her.'

She sat back and looked at the sweet peas again.

'It was a shock that. Nasty shock. But there I was with three babies and the farm and I thought he was bound to feel a bit left out of things and got lonely.

'It took a little while to get to that way of thinking and he was up on a bed groaning and lying on his face. Then the Post came out Thursday morning as usual.'

'Father was here then. I was in the Air Force. Remember that? We did National Service.'

'I remember.' She smiled and looked thoughtful.

'And the Post came out that Thursday,' he said.

'Ah yes. Well, there was a little bit about Adam Stong being shot in a gun accident on the farm. Just the usual. Then that night, a girl came to the kitchen door in a terrible state. I don't suppose she was more than seventeen. In tears and her belly out like a ship's sail.

'It was a difficult meeting, because she thought her promised had been shot dead and she was six months gone by him. It didn't occur straight away that her promised was my bloody husband. You don't. Somehow you just sit there and shake your stupid nut and say, "Impossible. It couldn't be." And you're telling *yourself* this, not somebody else...

'Well, that happened just about the end of the first year with him, Eddy. Dolly came as usual and after I'd told my husband if he went near when she was there I'd put the gun to his head next time.

'And I was in the mood then, to do it. Both barrels, slow motion, one after the other.

'But my father was always a strict man on

14

everybody but himself, and he'd always taught me that once I'd chosen my man, I had to stick. He brought me up, you know. Of course we had women there; you probably remember some of them, but he taught me all about farming and life—what he could remember of life outside farming. You learn something for a long time it gets into you and it gets a part of you. You don't obey; it gets what you have to do, and then what you want to do.

'Then years after, when it got worse, the boys were just about old enough to go, and they went, just to get away from Adam.

'I've gone on long enough. That's my epitaph and there's a good many more women than me who'll be pleased to see it.'

He looked at her very affectionately and shook his head, and there was a sadness about his eyes.

'I can't do it, Mamsie. I'll just leave out any mention. That's the best way.'

She cocked her head and looked at him critically. Then she took Jamey's paper from her bosom and held it out to him.

'That's what I wished for the stone,' she said. 'Jamey won't do it, either.'

He read almost in one blink, and then laughed.

'My dear girl! of course he won't do it!' He saw her smile and it took him back years to when she had looked just like that at him and, when his heart had got to a melting state, she had kicked him on the shin.

'He is right, you know,' he said, earnest again. 'It would cause scandal, Mamsie.'

'Scandal! I've been holding my ears against hearing that for years. I must have looked the biggest silly woman that ever lived in these parts, looking as if I didn't know what was going on.'

'I understand too well how you feel about that, Mamsie.'

'There's all sorts of ways for me to feel about it before it's all done, Eddy. And a good epitaph is the way to make it all clear and clear me, too.'

She took Jamey's paper. Eddy caught her hand, squeezed it and held on.

'It's for you, Mamsie. It's long ago I told you I loved you for the first time. It's many times I've told you since, but then you wouldn't have any of it. I tell you again today—'

'No man loves that long without having,' she said to her captured hand.

'It is because I do love you still that I ask you to tear those papers up and forget them.'

He let her hand go. He looked firm and angry but quite sure of his stand.

'It's kindness to me,' she said, 'by not doing what I ask?'

He got up and began to walk up and down.

'The inquest is over,' he said. 'A verdict of Accidental Death has closed it all. He has gone now. Just have his name, his birth and death on the stone and let that be all he gets.'

She looked at him.

'Will you tell me why I'll not be allowed to kill the legacy he left me?'

'He's dead! Let him lie. Don't let his poison make more trouble!'

'How can it do that?'

He stopped walking and looked at her.

'Because it might be dangerous!' he said.

She was surprised, then began to laugh.

'Oh, you must be a dramatic man, Eddy. I remember you always were. You remember you used to say, "O swear not by the moon, the inconstant moon—"?'

'Its' not the moon I'm worried about now, Mamsie, It's the inconstant bloody public!'

'Are they the dangerous ones?'

'They always are.'

CHAPTER TWO

1

It was a short journey across the Square from the offices of the Post to those of Jasey, Mellow, Mellow and Durr, solicitors and Commissioners for Oaths. Philip Jasey, a partner and one time schoolfriend, was expecting Mamsie.

Philip was quite a small, slightly rotund man with a multitude of faces put on to suit his assorted clients. The expressions ranged from

17

grave to hopeless on one level, and from mischievous to cheerfully dishonest on the lower and more profitable plane.

With Mamsie he was just pleased to see her and prepared to listen to her while sitting on a radiator under the window looking out over the town Gardens.

Philip was the third of Mamsie's circus which in her young days she had played like a team of horses. Philip was now married with two children.

Mamsie's range of friends had been, from the start, of the merchant and professional families because her late father, Jasper Willis, had been a hard man, a good farmer, and a staggeringly astute businessman. His own farm was always run on the old traditional lines, consequently the county papers never tired of putting in pictures of his activities and animals.

Such a farm attracted visitors. They brought their children to see the sort of farm that was in the picture books and there were rides on the haycart and other entertainments for which the farmhands charged a small fee and so relieved Jasper of the need of paying too much in wages.

He had bought land, sold it, rented it, worked it and did everything with it but lose money on it.

His wife had died when Mamsie was two and she had been brought up by a nurse who lived at the farm but nursed everybody in the area; a

18

renegade schoolmistress who had a passion for piglets and Jasper; the cook and butter maker who also fancied Japser; and the cowman, smith, wheelwright, thatcher and any other resident or itinerant artist who would spin her a yarn.

Jasper, aware of his power and reputation, accepted all the admiration, praise and outright feminine flattery due to his acumen, physical aspect and money, by sitting still with his eyes half closed.

Sometimes he went to Chapel. Other times he sent the message, 'God must wait till next week, haymaking.' He instructed his daughter in the ways of the Christian and himself obeyed as many of those ways as he thought fit or convenient.

Once a week he donned his boots, polished leather gaiters, breeches and hacking jacket and went to market on a horse which sometimes came back by itself.

In due season Mamsie was sent to the Girls' High School in the town which was strategically placed next to St Asaph's, a boys' school. Mamsie did not fish over the wall for boys, but it seemed like it.

When she was twelve Jasper died, but he had spent much time instructing her in the wiles of buying, selling, the qualities of stock and the ways of raising it, crops and the rest, but above all, the books and accounts and the various ways of balancing for maximum personal benefit.

Thus, with the guidance of the senior Jasey and an aunt Jessie who came in as a guardian, Mamsie began to manipulate the farm business with much of her father's skill. But for the duenna activities of Lessie Mamsie became her own mistress at fourteen.

It had been a shattering blow locally when the foreigner, Stong, arrived. Mamsie was eighteen when she invented the idiotic idea of drawing straws for her hand.

All these bits of pictures of their youth passed through the solicitor's mind as he squatted on the radiator and listened to what she had to say of the morning's difficulties.

'Have you got the papers with you?' he said, getting up and holding out his hand.

She gave them. He read them, gave a sudden short almost hysterical laugh, and then looked reprovingly at her.

'They're right, Mamsie. You can't do this sort of thing. I understand the feelings, but this is putting in the boot.'

'It's closing the account,' she said. 'I've paid all his debts.'

'You should have divorced him years ago,' Philip said.

'It's not in the Book of Willis,' said Mamsie. 'And by the way, I'm going back to my name. Do I have to sign a deed poll?'

'It would bring me in a small fee,' he said, rubbing his hands together, 'but it's quite unnecessary. You can choose any surname you like so long as there is no intent to evade creditors or indulge in criminal activity. Anyhow, Willis is your own name. But it's this epitaph business. Take my advice; forget it.'

'Eddy said it would cause a lot of rumours. But the rumour is dead and buried.'

'Old bones sometimes rattle,' he said. 'You know what people are for making things up about others.'

She sat back and watched him keenly.

'You do know what actually happened that night, do you?' she said.

'I know what the inquest decided, and that's all that matters. I believe, myself, that you covered some things up for his sake. So why do this now?' He held up the sheets of paper.

'What do you think happened that night?' she said calmly.

'What we were told. He was so drunk and wanted more Scotch so he went out in the Land-Rover wearing only his shirt, lost the way, went through the fence and over Gull cliff and finished upside down on the beach.'

'He thought he was being followed.'

'That was a drunken misapprehension. It was Gull light on the headland flashing. He thought it was a car.'

'They made nothing of it.'

'Well, they made a drunkard's dream of it and let it go at that.' He returned her watchful stare. 'What more than that did happen?'

21

'He wasn't home that night. He hadn't been home two nights. He took my truck to get the service done and never went near Joe Ellis with it. He went straight over to Landivet to Jessie Holmes with bottles of Scotch and they carried on two days while Jim was away upcountry seeing his folks about a legacy he never got.

'Well, Jim came back that night and found 'em together, and there was hell to pay. Jim was going to bash him to small pieces and this noble hero threatens him if he does he'll bankrupt him for the money Jim owed *me*.

'Me! I wouldn't push Jim for a farthing, and less than that would I have let that sod collect money for me.

'Well, he managed to get out to the Land-Rover, just in his shirt and Jim was coming after him, but he got off just in time.

'He thought Jim would follow in his car he'd just arrived in and chase him up. No doubt of that. So he skids off round the cliff road to try and lose Jim. Then he sees the lights behind him and goes over the cliff in panic.

'He died nobly, drowned in his own booze. But you knew that. He was broken about but he wouldn't have died but for all that drink choked him.

'Just in passing, I got the truck back this morning. Joe Ellis did a good job on it. Cost me five hundred and fifty quid. Do you know why it cost me? Because my husband took the insurance cheque, cashed it in the pub and

22

bought all the Scotch he took over to Jessie's.'

She was quite calm still.

'I didn't know about Jim,' Philip said.

'It was my idea that nobody would. It wasn't right to drag them into an inquest and all that dirt coming out. So I said he was on a bout at home.'

'That was generous, Mamsie. But all the more reason that you should let things die away on their own, not stir anything now.'

She kept looking at him.

'But how could it affect me badly? Because Jim saw me before he went home that night?'

Philip started.

'Did he?'

'Just dropped in to say he hadn't got far with his money, but he offered me so much now and again. You know. Postdated cheques and that. I won't have that. He's honest. He comes to see you when he owes. Most of 'em skulk as if you done them a wrong.'

'He didn't ask where your husband was?'

'Of course he didn't. I was long past letting him have a finger in any business of mine. Jim knew that, well as they all did.'

'Did you know about him and Jessie?'

'I knew it was somebody, because it always was. He sponged on her, even with her husband working hard and being hard up for people to pay him. Adam had no conscience.'

Philip walked back to the radiator, and turned round.

'Why didn't you divorce him years ago, when the boys went?'

'I said; tis not in the Book of Willis that I was taught.'

'Is it in the Book of Willis that you publish these epitaphs now?'

'Of course it is. Don't you remember my father?'

'I do. He used to frighten me to death. He pointed at me one day and said, "Fear God, boy!" I said my prayers for a week after that. But he's been gone a long time now.'

Then he thought of something.

'Did you come on business, Mamsie?' he said.

'Just one thing. About a will.'

'As I recall, he wasn't concerned in your will.'

'Not mine—his.'

'Was there a will?'

'It was a paper—part of a letter amongst his things. It was torn up. He must have dropped a bit and it went into the drawer with other things. It wasn't till after I thought it might refer to a will.'

'Have you got it?'

'No. I think it got thrown away. There was a good clear out. Things were in a mess. It was a torn up piece and it said, as I can remember, "you will benefit from" and on the line, under, "it is with Stevens and". Does that sound like talking about a will?'

'It could be. Well, we can easily find out if he went to a solicitor name of Stevens and Somebody.'

'I would like you to find out, Philip, because I don't want any ends hanging over. I want the whole lot cut and done with.'

'I'll do that, Mamsie. This afternoon. What about lunch?'

'I'm meeting Eddy at the Bull. You come as well, Philip. He suggested it. We can all talk, but if you gang up on me I'll bang your heads together and go home.'

'Agreed.'

She went. There was half an hour before meeting at the Bull. Philip rang Eddy.

After the preliminaries Philip said, 'We can't let her put out any adverse comment, you know.'

'I do know. It could mean lethal publicity. An awful lot has been kept quiet about the dear boy's life style and involvements, and if it did start coming out in some authentic guise, it could explode.'

'She doesn't realise the position, quite. That's my impression.'

'Mine is she does, and she's ready to challenge it. One just can't do that. It isn't worth the risk.'

'Exactly. Time is the factor. Let time go by and the cure's over. But she is in an awkward mood at the moment. It's difficult but we must play it broadly, don't you think?'

'Either broadly, or with a bludgeon. We'll play it as it goes. See you at quarter to.'

2

Millie was in the farm kitchen giving Harry tea. The morning had brought forth increment from the sow he had slept close to. Harry's mind was therefore at ease.

On being told to get back under the pump before he came in, Harry did so. The old pump was in full view of the kitchen window and Harry obliged by taking off everything and having a good scrub.

Millie watched now and again as she got the tea.

'It's time you put some fat on, Harry,' she said.

'I can do what I wants with what I got,' he said, and grinned. 'Missus not back?'

'She had a lot of business to do.'

'Fine woman, she. You know she'm having the horses back on the farm? For work?'

'Yes. That'll bring the visitors gawping.'

'And every gawp's a penny in me pocket. Four shires she'm having now to go with old Bess. Get rid of them bloody tractors, I hope. Well, that was a good tea, Mill. You're learning fast, girl.'

'I'll thump you!'

He laughed and she thumped him and he got her round the middle and proceeded to squash her till she couldn't breathe.

26

'I could do you a power of good, my girl,' he said.

A knocking at the front door broke up the wrestle. Millie shoved him aside and went through the office room to the front door.

A man stood there. A tall, smoothly dressed town man, Millie reckoned. He held a soft hat with which he fanned his face.

'I understand that Mr Stong has died,' he said, with an easy smile.

'That's right. Some days back now. What was it you wanted?'

'I wonder if Mrs Stong would see me?'

'She'm not in yet. She'm not calling herself to Stong any more, but her right name, Willis. What name is it I'll give when she's back?'

'Marks. Charles Marks.'

'Will you be back tomorrow then? She'll be at home tomorrow for sure.'

'Yes. I'll call again.'

'What business will it be about? She'm pretty well fixed up for seeds and that.'

'I'm nothing to do with seeds. My business is to do with Mr Stong's demise.'

'His what?'

'His sudden death.'

'Oh, well if it's to do with him, you have to put it to the lawyers in the town, here—' she turned and took a seed order form from the table by the door. 'That's their name and place.'

He looked at it, then brought a silver pencil

27

and small diary from his breast pocket and copied the information.

'That will be useful, but I shall have to see Mrs er, Willis,' he said. 'I shall be back tomorrow. Thank you.'

He smiled so that she thought he was really laughing at her, and turning, went away down towards the lane.

Funny, he didn't have a car, she thought. All the travellers have cars.

She turned and went back into the kitchen where Harry was standing close to the door post.

'You've been listening again!' she said.

'Twas worth the listenen,' he said. 'I see that bugger nosen about today. Over the farm. Round the barns he was. I went along to see what he was at but he walked out into the road. I reckoned he came in for natural causes, like, and so he walked on.

'Then I sees him again this afternoon, down by the stables. Looken up to the house he was. I couldn't go then. I was seeing to Queenie and just comed out for a fag. Had to go back and see she was proper otherwise I'd have gone after the bugger.'

'Did any of the others see him? Bert and Ivor?'

'They were down River Field maken up that hedge cows got through this mornen.'

'They'll be late for tea, then.'

'The way they're goen at it they'll be in for

tea breakfast time.'

Millie sat down.

'Funny, that man. Right smooth, he was. You feel he's got something on you. You know what I mean?'

'No. After that dear departed nobody's getting anythen on me again. You know he tipped me a quid, couple of weeks ago?'

'Bloody miracle.'

'He borrored two the week after, and he's took it to the grave with him. I aint raisen my hat to no sods like that.'

'Come on, Harry, he didn't know he was going to die.'

'He might have had a good guess, the way he was sitten on folk. I wonder she aint done it years ago.'

'You mustn't say things like that.'

'You're old fashioned, you are.' He pushed his cup across for more tea. 'Dessay a lotter folks think the same as me.'

'Well, she did have cause, lord knows.'

'When it got about he was dead in her truck, I heard some queer things about their wonderens and that, I tell you. All about her sawen through the steeren box and that. Not that they weren't on her side, mind you. No. Plenty of em wished they'd done it theirselves.'

'Well, they can't say things like that now, not after the inquest and everything.'

'They'll say anything any time, so long as they can get a bit er juice out of it.' He drank tea

29

and looked up. 'I reckon that matey was a spy.'

'What would anybody be spying for here?'

'I dunno, but he might have thought of somethen. You never knows what people's after till they've stole it from you.'

'It was about *his* death. That's what the man said.'

'I heard that. I pricked up me ears sharpish, I did. On account of what I was just talken about, folks talken of them steeren boxes and things.'

'That inquest settled all that. Twas nothing to do with her. Nothing at all.'

'Well, us knows that, you knows that and I knows that and all God's chillen got noses,' he said.

'Shut up! You're always the same. Wait till I'm right worked up and then say stupid things! Go on out! Back to work.'

'Girl, I'll have you know I times me work to the correct postures so no clocks is necessary nor any yapping females neither.' He got up and pushed his chair in to the table. 'But I says it again, that matey was a spy.'

'Oh yes, he's a spy but you don't know what he was spying for because there's nothing here to spy on.'

'Well, then,' said Harry, in a flesh-creep attack, 'Perhaps he weren't quite a spy, now, but a detective.' He grinned.

She pushed him towards the door.

'Go on! Out!'

He went. She turned back to the table. 'A detective? What's people talking about, then? No. He's ribbing me. Maybe it was he was hoping to buy the place. We do get a few now and again, looking round and that.'

Mamsie did not come back until five o'clock. She threw her straw hat on the desk in the farm room and came into the kitchen.

'I don't think I can stick biking like I used to, Mill,' she said. 'My bum's sore. Is that tea fresh?'

'I'll just make more,' Millie said, and quickly began to bustle. 'A man called for you. About the death. I showed him the lawyer's address but he said he'd come back tomorrow.'

'What did he look like?'

'A bit sinister. Like a villain.'

'Millie! too much telly!' Mamsie laughed. 'Charles Marks, you say? Marks?' She snapped her fingers. 'Adam mentioned a Marks once. Some kind of relative. Oh dear. I hadn't thought of relatives.'

'Well, none came for the funeral.' Millie sounded indignant.

'No.'

'Did you have a nice day?'

'Nice, but angry-making. A lot of stupid men kept stopping me from doing what I wanted.'

'Perhaps you were being naughty again.'

'They were being obstinate and silly.'

'What—all of them?' Millie smiled and

turned away to the teapot.

'Don't you start as well!' She looked to the door. 'Has Queenie farrowed?'

'Yes. And the cows got out down at River field.'

'On the road again?'

'Yes. No accidents. Twas all right. That's all, 'cepting this man calling. Harry said he saw him wandering about the farm on his own. Twice.'

'Whereabouts?'

'Once at the barns, then somewhere down by the pigs.'

'Didn't he ask anything?'

'First time Harry saw him he pushed off. Second time Harry couldn't go after him. It must have been a good time after that he knocked on the door here. So he must have been wandering about best part of the day.'

Mamsie frowned.

'Oh well, we shall find out what he wants tomorrow.'

'Sam picked up the cream early,' she said. 'There's quite a few visitors about, he said.'

Mamsie sipped her tea. The news of a stranger hovering about the farm seemed, after the day's frustrations, to put a black cap on her spirits.

The phone rang. She took her teacup into the farm room with her.

'It's Jim Holmes here, Mamsie. Sorry to disturb, but I've had a rather curious sort of a character here asking a lot of questions about your late husband.'

'Oh? When?'

'Not long ago. I thought I'd ring you and ask if he'd been there. Name of Marks, he said.'

'Yes, I didn't see him, but he did call. Did he say so?'

'No. Oh he called there earlier, did he? That's a bit odd.'

'Why?'

'Well, I said—I was a bit on edge, you'll guess, with questions about that, what happened—anyhow, I said if he was interested to go and see you. He didn't say he'd called there already.'

'And this was only a little while ago?'

'Twenty minutes. I thought I'd let you know because he was asking questions about Adam—and things. It was an odd way he had. It made me wonder what he was up to. So I rang to warn you. Now you say he's been there already. Don't you think it's—well, strange?'

'I think it's nasty,' said Mamsie. 'Take no notice. I'll see him tomorrow and put a flea right inside his ear.'

CHAPTER THREE

1

Samuel John Couch was a good gravedigger and keeper of the churchyard. He was also a

33

poet much respected on both sides of the Atlantic and made his main living by breeding Irish Setters.

On the sunny afternoon of the day Mamsie cycled into the town, Sam was down to grave bottom for a customer due at eleven-thirty the next morning. The recipient had left a widow, a mistress, a favourite lady cousin, five other cousins, a sister, five nephews, two nieces and a brother, all mean and grasping and ready to sprint a quarter mile at the drop of a copper coin.

'Quite a crowd, there'll be, regarding each other with the bitter acids of suspicion dripping on the coffin lid, all wiping their feet ready for the race back for the best seat at The Reading of the Will.'

A motor bike stopped out by the lych gate, and a clerical gentleman came in, black suit and dog collar curiously set off with a bone dome, as if he were about to take off into space for a personal call on God.

He took the helmet off as he came towards the grave.

'Hello, Sam,' he said.

'Hello, Charles. Well, now, what brings you over to the rival parish?'

'A mutual friend, dear boy. An old love.'

'I can guess,' said Sam clambering out of the hole. 'News spreads like spilt ink on the bedlinen as the shaking hand scrawls the end of

34

the will. You know, life would be a bargain if we didn't have to have an end to it.'

'You are an agnostic owl, Sam.'

'Come across and have a pot of tea. The dogs'll be glad to see you.'

'It's time you married a good woman,' said Charles.

'Good at what, I ask myself,' said Sam, putting on his jacket.

They went through the churchyard and across the field by the elm hedge to the cottage on the edge of a wood beyond. A few of the dogs barked but in the forest of waving silky tails it was difficult to tell which.

The vicar of Elbury was well known to the dogs and they appeared as the reason for the bulge in the right jacket pocket, which was full of dog biscuit, which he scattered to the flock.

Sam put on a kettle and brought out half a large plum cake. Mrs Garsen, who cooked for Sam and the dogs, was very good at plum cakes and once Sam had said they were good had committed himself to plum cakes for life at least once a week and sometimes twice.

'How are things on the Somerset border?' Sam said.

'Regrettably dry. It's time the old tabus were buried and we were allowed to have a pub. But I came to talk about Mamsie.'

'I know that. Everybody's talking about Mamsie. You'll be going to see her?'

'That's my main purpose. I'm on a couple of

free days and I shall stay with Fred tonight at the vicarage. He told me about her on the phone. Of course, he's not one of *us* but he's very fond of her.'

'Who isn't, to be fair? Among men, to be fairer still. Sometimes I get the impression women don't really like each other.'

'The bottom is going to boil out of that kettle, Sam.'

Over tea the subject narrowed.

'Would you have heard a suggestion around that the inquest was rigged in her favour?' the vicar said.

'You know what people are. Envious. It's the fashionable sin, envy.'

'Then you have heard it. But there must be a basic reason for it starting. I know the details of the death and I can't see any reason to doubt the verdict.'

'The rumour is that it didn't all come out. Something was covered up.'

'But his last hours are such a simple sequence of events, what could possibly have been left out?'

'The rumour is he didn't leave home that night, but some time before, though why that got about I can't say. It must have some strength to carry Somerset-far.'

'I told you, Fred phoned me.'

'Where did he get it? People don't usually pass on proper gossip to the vicar. This rumour has all been whispered. It's one of those hiss campaigns.'

'Well, he picked it up, anyway, so it must have come into the open in the course of a few hours. Almost as if some bad tongue knew the result of the inquest before it happened.'

'It's always possible to take bets on the results of an inquest.'

The Reverend Charles Brown sat back and looked at the ceiling beams.

'Something must have been known,' he said. 'If the rumour is that he left home a long time before it was said he did, then it sounds as if somebody knew where he had been in that missing time.'

'Mamsie said he was on one of his benders and always shut himself up for that. Of course, she didn't say bender, she said to work on something, though there was never any evidence of him doing any work any time in his natural. He was a dedicated follower of Karl Marx.'

'A wild Socialist?'

'No, a born sponger. Marx sponged for thirty years; Adam did twenty-five, as far as we know. I suppose you have heard of Adam's hobbies?'

'Very sad. But there was no doubt he was on a bender when he killed himself?'

'None at all. He was so full of the stuff the medicos said he actually choked himself after he fell.'

'Well, certainly no one else could do that for

37

him. The man was a rogue. It was that pagan business of the straws that caused this whole unhappy business.'

'To be fair, she did have five of us yowling after her and none of us proposed an honest woman until that drab swindler came from wherever it was, then when he proposed we all thought of the same thing.'

'We were a lot of bloody idiots,' said the vicar. 'Have you got any of your blended tobacco? I was looking forward to the scrounge of a pipeload.'

Sam got the jar and put it on the table.

'Jamey was in the churchyard early afternoon,' he said. 'Brought in a curb for the Collison girl. Don't like curbs. Difficult to cut up to with a mower.'

'And Jamey? Well, is he?'

'Fine, but bothered. Mamsie wanted him to cut something scandalous on the tombstone.'

The vicar stopped filling his pipe and stared.

'You're not serious.'

'Jamey was. Worried. He told it to me because it was a little poem in memory of the dear departed. It even rhymed lecher with betcher. It would have rocked 'em in the aisles, that one. I don't quite remember it, but I do remember that.'

'Lecher? On a gravestone? A headstone? A memorial?'

'That's what he was, Charles. Lecher, boozer, twister, swindler—and I'm not sure that was all, either.'

'The fellow's dead. Leave him. Our trouble is with the living. What possessed her to go to Jamey with a thing like that? Has he told anybody else?'

'No. He told me because I was one of the Mamsie consortium, and I suppose now we must consider her as our limited liability.'

'It's odd that while he was alive and causing her trouble, she caused us to be unable to do anything; now he's dead, and we ought to do something, she's causing the trouble.'

'Well, that's Mamsie,' said Sam, and grinned.

'That's very true,' the vicar said, and laughed.

'Which reminds me, a stranger came into the yard this morning when I was working,' Sam said. 'He went to Stong's grave and then came back and said, "Not many flowers there". I said, "The widow's. That's enough." Then he grinned, or I could say leered, being fond of melodrama.'

'Was he just looking around? Church visitor?'

'He just came in the gate, went to that grave, looked, spoke to me and went. He came to see that grave. It's all he did see.'

The vicar got up and pocketed his pipe.

'I think I'll drop in on Mamsie now and see you later. Fred knows I'll be late.'

'I was wondering if that fellow was smelling

out something,' said Sam idly, 'to do with the rumours, or because of.'

The vicar looked at the open door, then back at Sam.

'It's very easy to be a coward over some things,' he said. 'I've been meaning to ask you since we sat down, but the courage wouldn't come. But now you mention the stranger in that way—'

'I'll have a guess on the question,' Sam said, 'But you put it first.'

'Is there any slight possibility that murder could have been done?'

'I would have won the bet,' Sam said. 'But it's best to bear in mind that once folk get hot in the mind about a scandal, then anything's possible to them, and the trouble with talk is it may have no substance when it starts, but it takes a damn lot of clearing up.'

'You didn't answer my question, Sam.'

'No. I didn't. You talk of slight possibilities. I was never quite able to sort out in my mind just what murder is, but there is a possibility that Adam Stong didn't drive over the cliff because he was cross-eyed drunk.

'There was some suggestion that some other car was chasing him and he went through the fence trying to get away from it.'

'How did anyone know another car was there? There were no witnesses.'

'They did not know, Charles. It came up when they were trying to find reasons for him going through the fence and then on over the cliff.

'The fence, you might remember, is twenty yards from the edge because of danger of cliff falls thereabout.'

'And the shock of hitting the fence should have brought him to his senses? I see. If he had been plain drunk that crash should have been enough to make him stand on the brake, I suppose.'

'Well, to make him swerve somewhere, not just go straight on. That's what the discussion was.'

'It does leave a gap where something could have happened, Sam.'

'It was dark that night. He might have seen a light behind, but judging from his tracks it was the light on the Point, flashing on. That was accepted and that part was dropped.'

'Otherwise there was a car behind, chasing him. If he had left home hours before then what he did in the interim could have provided the car and motive for a chase.'

'Of course. But it was Mamsie who said he had gone out not so long before he went over.'

'Thus putting herself in a position where, if anyone was accused of having chased him to his death, it would be she.'

'Except that there wasn't another vehicle on the farm that night but two tractors and a combine harvester, none of which could have paced the vehicle over the cliff.'

The vicar went to the door, and eager snuffles from hopeful walk-eager dogs started up.

'Not now, dogs,' the vicar said. 'Make way for The Maker's rep.'

2

The Reverend Charles Brown arrived at the farm on his motor bike at milking time. Mamsie was doing the milking as Harry was late mucking out the horse and he talked to the horse so long he didn't notice the time till the cows started bellowing.

The vicar found her in the milking shed. She was clearly busy but delighted to see him and asked questions about his wife and family while she inspected the condition of her cows.

'You'd look better in a mob cap, sitting on a stool and pulling the pumps in the traditional manner,' he said.

'Well, it's sometimes necessary, but this unglamorous machine is quicker, whatever else. Are you on holiday?'

'Two free days,' he said. 'I called in on Sam on the way.'

'Dear Sam,' she said. 'You know he does that gravedigging as a sort of penance for not being a believer.'

They both laughed, and she looked at him sharply.

'You've come about something serious, I guess,' she said. 'Have you?'

42

'Just to see you, and talk, Mamsie.'

'You look as if you're hopping about on top of a wire hedge,' she said and went to the shed door. 'Harry, leave the horse and come and take over. I've got business.'

They went in to the farm room after she'd kicked off her boots on the step.

'Now,' she said, 'if you're going to lecture me, Charles, I shall lock you in with the bull.'

'My dear girl, don't be so suspicious. In a way you're right. It is about Adam Stong and it is about that night.'

'How do you know about it all? Right away up-country where you are?'

He kept Fred out of it by saying he had come into the home town that morning and people had talked to him and so forth.

'There are bad rumours going around and it upset me,' he said.

'Well, don't bother yourself with that rubbish. I don't.'

'Don't be stupid, Mamsie. All things are worth bothering about if they can cause damage.'

'Yes, Father Charles Brown MA.'

'Don't make fun. I'm serious. The gossip is concerned with what happened to the deceased in the few hours before he died.'

It would normally be difficult for him to refer to the departed by anything but the name used by the bereaved, but he had known her and the story too long not to mistake her

43

wish now.

'Yes, I know. But it's nobody's business. The inquest finished with it all. No need to bother.'

'Mamsie, inquests may be re-opened if evidence turns up from any quarter which shows clearly that some error may have occurred at the first hearing, due to that evidence having been omitted.'

'Is that so?' she said. 'Well, I shan't go. I shall just say I've seen it already.'

'Mamsie!'

'I know I'm being foolish, Charles, dear, but really I am sick to death of it all. He went over the cliff and died. That's all that matters.'

'Surely you realise that by spreading a rumour about that the evidence wasn't all there, it could give rise to a worse rumour, that it was murder and not an accident?'

'That's too far-fetched. How in hell could anyone have got near him? Or do you mean somebody else started the Land-Rover going and then jumped out?'

He started slightly.

'I confess I didn't think of that,' he said. 'I suppose that is possible.'

For the first time she realised that perhaps she had made a serious mistake, but until that moment of saying it, the picture of such a thing happening had never come into her head.

She realised that murder would have been possible with a man so drunk he had even drowned himself in the stuff; he would have

44

made no resistance. He probably wouldn't have known what was going on if somebody had half got in and started it driving towards the cliff.

'But there is a snag,' said Charles. 'Once again—the fence. I don't see how anyone could have hung on to the side while deliberately smashing through a wooden fence. It would very probably smash him off as the car went through.'

She felt relieved, as if she had nearly been accused of murder.

'No, of course he wouldn't. And there's no gate where he could have gone through and started on the other side. There's no gate at all in the fence.'

'Well, that settles that. What isn't settled is where he was before it happened, and I think you know where.'

'It doesn't help, Charles. It could just get an innocent person into the muck, and I won't have that.'

'A man?' he said suddenly.

'It is a man, yes.' She was surprised at his change of tone. 'Not a fancy one.' She shook her head.

'People might think otherwise if it should come out.'

'I'm working so that it won't come out.'

He got up and began walking about, trying to think.

'I wonder what started the rumour?' he said.

'Well, I haven't heard much of it. You never enjoy the gossip about yourself. But people tell me. Friends do. It's funny that nobody heard anything before the inquest, because a few days went by before that.'

'The hawks were probably hovering round the inquest hoping for tasty morsels which hadn't appeared before and were disappointed.'

'You mean they'd made something up and thought it would come out in the court?'

'Yes. When somebody well-known dies suddenly it becomes a big news feature locally, and things do get added, twisted about, cooked and doctored.'

He stopped pacing.

'Do you know of anyone who would wish you ill, Mamsie? Probably a woman. Someone you've known a long time.'

'If there is such a one, I don't know of her. I'm a busy woman. It's being busy with my work that made it liveable. If I hadn't had my farm and lots to do and had to live with him and nothing else, well then I could have murdered him.'

'Were you man and wife?'

'Not for years.'

'Do you think that was known?'

'Oh, he would have said so when it suited him.'

He looked out of the window at the gathering dusk.

46

'Have you had any visitors today?'

'There was a man, but I was out. Why? I get many travellers here, salesmen. For sure I don't go to find them. This man was about Adam's death. He said he would come back tomorrow.'

'There was a man at the grave today, so Sam told me. It could have been the same one. Or have there been others?'

He looked very sharp, then relaxed as she shook her head.

'In any case, I'll send them to Philip Jasey. I'll send this one, too.'

'Yes, that's best. Philip knows the safe way of dealing with unknown callers.'

'What's this *safe* business, Charles? Safe from what, if you please?'

'It means that I hear you've been behaving very unsafely. Sam told me about the epitaph. That surely was pushing it a bit far, Mamsie?'

She sat stiffly.

'I will not argue about my feelings and what is needed for balm.'

'Then let me ask you a question. You have already made it clear that you are embittered, but think back to the beginning of the year.'

'This year?'

'Yes. If he had died then would you have wished the same epitaph, or has something happened in the last few months that was worse than anything that went before it?' She looked at him squarely.

47

'Now there's a question,' she said.

'If it isn't easy, it doesn't matter,' he said.

She looked at him with an open, splendid look which took his memory back through the years to when that same glorious innocence had presaged any old barefaced lie that had come into her head.

'I've made it too easy for you,' he said, putting up his hand to stop her speaking. 'But I've known you long enough to know you're not a vicious or a vengeful person, so to me it seems essential that something happened before this which you discovered, not long before, or just after, the accident. What was it?'

'What sort of thing do you mean?' she said, innocence unblinking.

'A sort of thing which, when you found out, was such a shock to you that your previously convenience-adjusted view of him and his doings was suddenly jerked right off its tracks. What was it?'

'Well, it couldn't have been anything I noticed,' Mamsie said.

Charles sighed.

'We are your old friends. We want to help you. That is the reason I've come. Have you spoken to Philip, or Eddy?'

'I saw them both today,' she said and smiled, then made a comic gesture of what-does-it-matter? 'I had a brief sort of emancipation. I thought it was all over and though I couldn't—and wouldn't—go back and start again I could go back and start feeling again. I felt free, just for a little while.'

'You could make it for good. But if you hold bitterness in your heart it can never end at all. That is why I want to know what it is that shocked you so much.'

'It's over,' she said. 'He can't do any more to me now.'

Charles sat down facing her.

'That is just what he still can do,' he said quietly, firmly. 'Freedom is a state of mind and it cannot exist if you are still tied to something which you should leave behind. By feeling about it, you keep it with you.'

'Hell, don't you think I know that, Charles? It's just that I want to. It's just that I can't help wanting to. It's something I feel I ought to do. A duty.'

'I remember your father speaking like that when I was a boy. I was hiding in the barn. The vicar, Old Jason, was rowing with him, trying to make him change his mind.

'Then your father shouted, "For the good of the people of this parish, the sod must be stripped of all his pretence, his deceit and his villainy." Jason said, "It will kill him. He is a sick man. Have mercy." And your father said, "Mercy has to come from what *you* did, not from what others are prepared to do".'

Mamsie sat forward.

'And that's right for those who took all the mercy without paying by giving any back.'

'That isn't Christian, Mamsie.'

'It is. You always forget the Old Testament. There's a lot of religion in there, too.'

CHAPTER FOUR

1

The reverend visitor thought he had better change tactics. He had no intention of being led into theological arguments. He remembered from years ago how easily Mamsie could lead conversations round to what she wanted to talk about.

She was specially good at it when being accused of some evil.

'I suppose the boys couldn't get back for the funeral,' he said.

'The boys had no reason to come,' she said. 'He drove them away so they stayed away.'

'I thought they would be concerned for you.'

'When he died, which was several days back, I sat down and wrote to the boys and told them how I was, how I felt, and what my circumstances were—which were better for his going—'

'Please!'

'Don't be niminy,' said Mamsie, firmly. 'I'm richer for his going, financially.'

'That was your doing. You insisted on paying for his misdeeds.'

'Because he was weak. I think that was what it was. I felt that if he was cut adrift, he would sink. I didn't want him to do that. I didn't want that I should feel sorry, or guilty, even.'

'You're making yourself out very badly, my dear!'

'I am very bad,' she said, with splendid composure.

'Why on earth do you say that?'

'Well, who's good? Present company excepted.'

'Mamsie, what was it you found out that made you so bitter after all these years?'

'I was bitter from the start. There never was just me, you know.'

'Yes. I know of the infidelities, but so did you. I imagine it was no secret.'

'He played on a woman's weakness,' she said. 'He was a poor lover. Even when he got what he wanted he was poor.'

Charles wondered whether she spoke from frustration or experience and shifted in his chair only seconds after he had sat down.

'But he was good fun on the surface?'

'He was good fun until he'd got the woman, then he was all pretended gloom and worry and wondering where he would get money to pay his debts and all that. He made a business of it.'

'Have you always known he got money from others?'

She looked at the window.

'I may have guessed.'

51

'But you didn't know?' He waited. 'Did you find this out recently?'

'I always knew it.'

The vicar was becoming more and more uneasy. The rumour seemed to have put her on the defensive so much so that she was fending off any suggestion of accepting help. She might think asking help might imply guilt.

'Charles, I wonder just what you are getting at?' she said quietly. 'Do you believe I have done something wrong—something important, that is?'

'No. But I think you are in danger of being accused of things you have not done. To fight that it's necessary to know what you *have* done.'

'There is a man coming up the lane,' she said, staring at the window. 'I wonder if this is the one who called about Adam's death?'

'What was his name?'

'Same as yours, but Marks. Charles Marks, Millie said. Do you mind if I see him alone?'

He got up, but hesitated. She looked up and laughed.

''Tis all right, Charles. I won't murder the poor man.'

'Take care, Mamsie. Take care.'

'Go out and talk to Millie. She likes handsome men.'

He went out just before the caller knocked on the door.

'Come in,' Mamsie said, and stood up.

The man opened the door and stood on

the step.

'Mrs Willis? Once Mrs Stong?' he asked, with a half smile.

'Yes. Come in. You called before I think and said you would call tomorrow. Why tonight?'

'I was passing.'

'Why were you passing?'

He was startled.

'I beg your pardon?'

'Why were you passing?' She spoke slowly and clearly as if he was deaf.

'I think that is my business.'

'I don't think it is.'

'But I—'

'You came to call here. You were not passing.'

'Very well. I came to call here.'

'Not a very good start—lying,' she said calmly. He looked at her curiously, apparently thinking of taking a different approach from the one he had had in mind.

'Why come at all? You were given the solicitor and his address.'

'My business is personal.'

'I have no personal business with strangers.'

'It concerns the death of your husband.'

'That is not personal. It is public.'

'What I have to say is personal. I don't wish to say it in public.'

'I have no business of that kind. Consult the solicitor. He will advise you.'

Charles Marks was losing his calm and

53

spoke sharply with a small show of teeth for greater clarity.

'I have information that your husband was murdered.'

'Then you should give it to the Coroner. He said he was not.'

Marks stood still. He was clearly angry but in control. The woman surprised him. He was unprepared for challenge with such assurance.

'You don't want to know what my information is?' he said.

'That's the part where you should have said, "Very well, I will do as you suggest and give it to the Coroner," and go.'

'I am not here to cause trouble, Mrs—Willis.'

'Very well. Then don't.'

Anger suddenly changed into a short snort of laughter, quickly brought under control.

'I seem to be losing ground,' he said.

She smiled.

'You never had any. What's the matter with the solicitor?'

'Nothing that I know of. I'm sure he would be most helpful, if this was the sort of help I wanted.'

'Surely you need help. You suggested I murdered my husband.'

'Not at all, Mrs—Willis. Such a thing is impossible.'

'How do you know what is possible?'

'You were here when he was killed.'

54

She sat down and looked up at him.

'You seem to know more than the Almighty. Even He doesn't know where I was.'

'It was proved at the inquest, without the proof being obtrusive or offensive.'

'You were at the inquest, Mr Marks?'

He inclined his head.

'I have the complete record. Everything that was said.' Curiously, he made it sound unimportant.

'Then your business, whatever it may have been, was ended with the verdict.'

'The crucial evidence did not come out at that hearing.'

'So why didn't you tell the Coroner? I think there is some law says you must or go to jail.'

They looked at each other.

'I don't believe in sending people to jail,' he said. 'Incarceration teaches nothing, solves nothing.'

'I always like a social reformer. They seem to think I ought to feel guilty.'

He looked at the hat he held.

'You're a very difficult woman to talk to,' he said.

'I should think so,' she said, looking frankly at him as he glanced up from the hat. 'That's the third new opening you've made in five minutes. You shouldn't have started with a lie. For me, that's the end.'

'You can't believe that I may have come to help you?'

'For heaven's sake! Why does everybody want to help me? I'm suffocating with helpers.'

'Not quite like this one,' he said. 'I can prove that your lover murdered your husband.'

She cocked her head and looked sharply at him.

'You must be the cleverest man that ever was. You make up a murder and now you make up a lover. I don't have one.'

He smiled, more at his ease.

'You'd hardly say otherwise,' he said.

'I could hardly, as you say. I'm not a liar. One lie means so many more and that makes me tired. Well, Mr Marks, if that is your personal burden, I wish you well with it. I'll just say it's worth nothing to me.'

'I asked for nothing.'

'Perhaps that's wise. That gun in the corner I keep loaded overnight.'

He looked.

'Do you always keep it there?'

'Unless I'm out shooting round the farm.'

'It wasn't there the night your husband died.'

She was surprised at last.

'Was it not? How was it I didn't notice it was missing—if it was.'

'You gave it to him and he killed your husband with it.'

'Goodness! And Adam ate the shot, I suppose? Funny the doctors didn't notice any pellets about him.'

56

'There were no pellets. The shots were blanks, fired from the side of the road so that Stong swerved off and through the fence.'

'In all twenty-five years the last thing I suspected of him was nerves. If he saw somebody trying to hit him from the roadside, he'd have driven at 'em—so long as he was in a good strong car, of course.'

'I have the cartridges,' he said.

'Then take them to the Coroner, as I said. But I'm thinking that if there is an arrest on account of this evidence, it'll be yours, not anybody else's.'

'Well, I won't take any more of your time,' he said, turning to the door.

'Oh, just one thing before you go.'

He turned back.

'Just what are you? Have you any connection with Adam Stong?'

'Half-brother.'

She just smiled.

'Good night, Mr Marks. Don't forget the solicitor in the morning. You'll surely need him.'

He went, quietly, and gave a polite nod of the head before closing the door.

2

At eleven next morning Charles Marks saw Philip Jasey in his office.

'We haven't met before,' Marks said. 'I am Adam Stong's half brother. I understand you act for Mrs Stong.'

'Yes. We did not act for her husband, though.'

'I called on her last evening. She asked me to see you about the matter. She said she was unable to help.'

'About what?'

'Adam's money.'

Philip stared.

'I understood he had none. There were his private possessions, of course, but no record of money affairs except Bank statements and correspondence. His private account. Nothing to do with the farm.'

'I believe that there was a considerable sum of money in his possession when he died.'

'Really? But surely any such asset would have come to light? The legal profession is usually aware of the results of inquests and I feel sure his solicitors would have come forward.'

'To the widow?'

'Of course.'

'I had thought that myself, however that doesn't seem to have happened. The bank statements and correspondence; were they favourable?'

'No.'

'It's possible, is it, that if a husband wishes his wife not to know in any circumstances, that only a named beneficiary would be informed of any residue?'

'Not really possible. No. But if it did happen by any underhand methods, then when it did come to light the whole lot could be claimed by the widow or her children.'

'You mean they would have to fight in the courts for it?'

'Yes.'

'But if the widow was well-off and refused to act to get such money?'

'In the case of Stong's widow, that is probably true, as far as she is concerned. But there are three sons by the marriage.'

Philip was very watchful.

'Yes, of course,' Marks said.

'What gave you the idea that your half-brother left any money, and in the way you imply?'

'I saw a letter which he wrote some time ago.'

'He wrote to you telling you this?'

'He wrote to my wife. A case of half-incest, perhaps. I was at that time suspicious of certain actions of hers and looked in her bag. I read so much and then she came in. The letter was burnt. This is all confidential.'

'You knew his writing?'

'More than that. I knew it was him she'd been seeing.'

'Have you spoken to her about it since his death?'

'Yes. Unfortunately she was not in the mood. She packed her bags.'

'This was before the inquest?'

'It was a week ago. I haven't heard from her since.'

'I see. Well, I don't see how we can help you, Mr Marks. We know of no money in his estate. Or do you suggest your wife went off under some pre-arrangement with the deceased?'

'Running away with his money, you mean?' Marks smiled quite pleasantly. 'She would enjoy that kind of elopement. It is possible, but you say there is no legal way in which money could have been hidden and taken by an accomplice without the legal beneficiaries knowing.'

'No legal way, no. It's possible, I suppose that your wife just went in the way of wives?'

'Very frank, Mr Jasey, but no. She was on a good wicket. I do quite well. I own a chain of general stores. They are profitable.'

'But The Spoilt Wife—the Sudden Exit, Tantrums. Instability.'

'She is stable in wishing to keep the means of a comfortable instability.'

'She thinks the best has gone out of marriage?' Philip was curious to know a good deal more about the visitor.

'She thinks the best of anything is something she hasn't had yet.' He frowned. 'I didn't know Mrs Stong was such an attractive woman. It surprised me.'

'You haven't met before?'

'No. Adam's story was always that he'd

left her.'

'You saw him regularly?'

'We saw a lot of him at one time, then I saw only a little and my wife saw the rest.'

'You didn't go to the wedding, then?'

'I was in Australia, making money which I afterwards invested in my shops here. Then I married. Several times I thought of divorce, but always opted for another try. After a while I became philosophical. I realised it was her way. She was a wanton. Nothing evil. Just that the spirit took her from time to time, and she always came back, so I got to accepting it.'

'Very generous, Mr Marks,' Philip said.

'Perhaps.'

'Well, Mr Marks, as you are a business man obviously you have your own solicitors.'

'Yes. But because I am up here for a few days I thought it possible you would know of any money which Adam might have given—by one means or another—to my wife. If she has got mixed up in something doubtful, I don't want it to be known locally, where we live.'

'Yes. I understand. But why do you say "something doubtful"? Was your half-brother likely to get involved in doubtful business?'

'He would have mixed in anything for a fast buck. Well, I mustn't take up more time. I am glad to have seen you. I came because I am in the district for a few days.'

'On business?'

Marks looked directly at Philip.

'No, sir. I have decided to try and find my wife.'

When he had gone, Philip rang Mamsie and told her Marks had been.

'Oh,' she said. 'I didn't think he'd go to you.'

'He seems to have an idea that Adam left money and that his wife knows about it.'

'What!'

'We haven't had any change from the enquiry yesterday about that name on the torn letter, but it's strange that he should have come about the same thing. I chatted him up to find out more about him.'

'He didn't say anything about money to me.'

'He said he did.'

'No. He just came to say he knew my lover had murdered Adam.'

It was Philip's turn to cry, 'What!' After a second, he said, 'Was his manner threatening?'

'No, no. He didn't really seem to know what manner to have. He was one thing, then another. Kept changing the approach ... Who do you think is here? Charles, the reverend and beloved.'

'Charles? Why's he come over? No, don't tell me. He's heard. Where is he? ... In the Vicarage? Okay. I'll drop in and see him. It's a while since he's been over. I must see you—Lunch? Yes. Right.'

Philip rang the Vicarage. Charles waited for him there. Greetings over, they talked.

'Last evening I spoke with her girl, Millie

62

and the cowman-general, Harry,' Charles said. 'Both were content, even pleased, with Adam's death. Harry even went so far as to say, "I wonder she didn't do it herself, fore now". That sort of thing could add fuel if someone starts a real fire.'

'They will,' said Philip. 'I think at first she had no idea what people were saying, but when she did hear, she got bloody-minded. That doesn't do when you're the football.'

'I have an idea,' said Charles, 'that the only way to settle this matter is to find out exactly what did happen that night.'

'Legally, we know. The inquest is closed. It takes a lot more than rumour or malicious gossip to reopen these matters, as you well know.'

'But as it stands, she is open to these attacks for ever. Such stories are always worth passing on until they become legends. "The Black Widow of Bloodstain Farm". You know the order of these things very well.'

Philip laughed and looked out of the window at the church.

'The man Marks is rather interesting,' he said. 'He says he believes his wife to be round here somewhere. But he also thinks she has come to get money Adam left and that's why she's here.'

'You surely don't mean Adam hid it?'

'Well, we must realise that he kept up the legend he had no money at all.'

63

'So it must exist in an unorthodox savings account—if it exists at all. Or do you imagine that the man Marks is after it, and the wife is a front for the operation, as they say?'

'If he were, I don't think he'd have made himself such a public figure.'

'As far as this so called murder goes; what is this about a lover?'

'I doubt there is one. Certainly not round here. She is discreet in personal things and I'm sure she would never put her foot in it locally. One can see now how quickly any such gossip would spread and it never has done. Marks, remember, is a stranger to this area.'

'Well, a woman needs affection and we know she had very little from the dear departed.'

'Don't get too wide-minded about it, Charles. I can't see Mamsie getting into any liaison tough enough to end in murdering the husband.'

'Mamsie—how did she get that name? What is it short for?'

'Nothing really. Remember the Aunt who came in as her governess when she was very small? Well, she'd come over from Brittany where she'd been in service, and she called the child Mamselle. The old man shortened it and there it stuck.'

'I never knew that—' He turned as someone came up the vicarage drive. 'Eddy! Is this a gathering of the clans?'

64

Eddy came in through the french windows having seen the two men in the room. He pulled a bunch of different notepapers from his pocket.

'Your office told me you were here,' he said, looking at Philip. 'And Charles too, that's fine. News spreads on its own without my paper, it seems.'

'What have you got there—letters?' said Philip.

'All anonymous, all on the same line. For instance:

'"Dear Sir,

Do you know Mamsy Stong got her husband murdered and nobody spoke at the inquest?"

'There are three spelling attempts at 'inquest", which I think is a mislead.'

'And the others are on the same lines?' Philip said.

'Let's go through them. There may be something familiar somewhere.'

CHAPTER FIVE

1

The letters were shared out amongst the three men and passed from one to the other without comment on the first reading.

'I class these five as a concerted effort,' Eddy

65

said, putting five in a pile. 'The other three seem to be individual.'

'I'm not sure about all five, but four, I should say, were the result of an initial talk-over,' Philip said.

'Yes, I think you are probably right,' Charles said. 'Each one of the four mentions the same thing; the fact that they know—or seem to know—Adam did not go to the cliff directly from his own home.'

'The last one,' Eddy said, picking it up, 'is the work of Lady Hoskins. Of that I am quite sure.'

'Let me see it again,' Philip said. He read it once more, then handed it back to the pile. 'Yes. You're right. I know that typewriter. She often writes to us threatening legal action against somebody or other. Action for libel, slander, defamation of character.'

'Is she over-sensitive?' Charles asked, with a faint smile.

'She is a managing whore,' said Eddy. 'Her husband left her some years back and she runs three girls, one of which is her daughter.'

'Quite openly?' Charles said, surprised.

'There's no law against such industry,' Philip said, 'except in that you must not offer it in the street.'

'I shouldn't have thought there was a market for call girls in this area,' Charles said.

Eddy laughed.

'The place is packed with holiday homes,

weekend cottages, and so forth,' he said. 'And her ladyship offers a quite special service. The girls are very presentable escorts. I can assure you, Charles, it is a sound business.'

'You think that Adam might have indulged?'

'I don't know about that.' Eddy was doubtful. 'He rather fancied getting paid for it than paying.'

'Seems rather odd that such a woman should write an anonymous letter about such things,' Charles said, walking away from the table. 'The others might well be tongue-waggers. We all have them, Lord knows, but a woman in such circumstances—' He shook his head.

'She has written to me often,' Eddy said. 'She is keen on conversation and keeping her name in the paper. She argues about footpaths, beach erosion, cliffs. Writes a good letter.'

'It sounds like supreme impudence,' said Charles. 'If as much is widely known about her as you suggest?'

'Titled tarts are rare and rather precious,' Eddy said, and laughed. 'This is away from the purpose.'

'I'm not so sure,' Charles said. 'If a woman such as you describe starts an action like this, there must be something more than a wish to see justice done.'

'It is curious,' Philip said. 'But is it likely to be any more dangerous than any of these others? I don't think so.'

'Of course, the police will have some,' Eddy said.

'They take little notice of anonymous letters,' Philip said. 'Most are malicious, and if one did seem cause for action it would be a very tricky matter to handle.'

'It may not produce action,' said Eddy, 'but it gets you noticed. That's the trouble.'

'It seems to me,' said Charles, 'that if we find out exactly what Adam did do that night, it would help squash all this.'

'Mamsie doesn't know,' Philip said. 'That is true to his form, because most of his life seemed to have been taken up by things Mamsie didn't know about until a long time after.'

'But she lied—just a little bit,' said Eddy.

'I've always found with her that she usually lies to protect someone, not for herself.'

'Hang on,' cautioned Eddy. 'She could lie to save herself being thought of as a fool.'

'Maybe, but there is nothing vicious in that,' said Charles.

'Let us see what we do know,' said Philip. 'Mamsie said Adam was at Jim Holmes' playing around with the wife. He came back and Adam bunked.'

'That was immediately before the crash?' Eddy said.

'We don't know that, do we?' Philip said. 'And when did he leave home? He was supposed to take the truck to Ellis's and didn't.'

'Then see when Ellis expected it in,' said Eddy. 'I'll ring him. Parish pays.' He went out to the phone in the vicarage hall, and came back.

'Well?' Philip said.

'It was expected the morning before the accident.'

'The morning before?' Charles said. 'That's thirty-six hours before anything happened. And he had the vehicle, so he could have gone anywhere.'

'We haven't police facilities for asking if anyone noticed vehicles going anywhere,' said Eddy. 'Frankly, I don't see how we can get on with this. If we go and ask Jessie Holmes if he said where were he'd been before he'd got to her we shall get a very short answer.'

'There is only one way it would be possible for us to find out anything about that missing time,' said Philip. 'And that's to assume Mamsie got him killed.'

Eddy laughed, but shortly. Charles tutted.

'And if we did find out,' said Charles, 'what could we do with the information?'

'It would be an armour against the growth of this sort of thing. This has sprung from the idea that it was no accident but a murder, and a murder which has not been spotted. That man Marks has been going about spreading ways and means of doing it, and when you think of it, the idea isn't impossible.'

'Philip, dear boy, speaking as a necessary

student of crimes of passion, I don't know of any one where the husband or lover has gone to lengths of planning and timing and thought for the future such as would have been essential for this one.'

'But if the motive is not jealousy?' said Charles.

'Then what?' said Eddy.

'Suppose there is money?' said Philip. 'Suppose he did have some somewhere?'

'If that's it, Mamsie phases out, because she has no need of money,' said Eddy.

'The difficulty we seem to be passing over,' said Charles, 'is the suggestion in all those letters, not that she murdered her husband, but that she had him murdered. That makes it more difficult to present a clear case of innocence.'

He went to the window and looked out.

'I would like to meet her ladyship,' he said, turning back.

'Charles, dear boy!' said Eddy and laughed.

'I want to know why she wrote such a letter,' Charles said, unmoved. 'So long as you're both quite sure she did?'

'The style and that old typewriter, yes,' Eddy said, and looked at Philip, who nodded. 'One of the girls could have used the typewriter, but they would never write just like this. Lesley was a gossip columnist before she hooked the Hoskins. She got wind he was going to get a ticket for supporting his party so earnestly, and

70

she wanted to be Lady Anybody so she acted.'

'The daughter is not Hoskins,' Philip said.

'A previous husband?'

'No, Charles. Not quite so definite as that.' He looked at his watch. 'I must get down to Mamsie. She said lunch.'

'How shall I put it to her ladyship?' said Eddy. 'A friend? You certainly don't look holy in that get-up, Charles. Right, a friend. And what excuse?'

'I leave it to you,' said Charles.

2

'Who the hell's that?' said Lady Hoskins, staring out of the french windows. 'Not Eddy—the man with him?'

Her daughter Elaine came to the windows and looked out.

'Nice looking,' she said, 'but he hasn't the wealthy look, somehow.'

'I mean, who is he? I seem to have seen him somewhere before.'

'Surely you don't remember *everybody* you've seen before, dear?' said Elaine, with a smile. 'Not by name?'

The maid came in.

'There's two men—oh, you've seen. One's off the paper, you know,' she said.

'All right, Lil. He owns the paper. Get some drinks. Friendly visit for sure—I hope.' She looked a little sharply at the car before she

71

turned and studied herself in the overmantel mirror.

She looked very beautiful, tall, cool, elegant.

'Sod off, darling,' she said. 'I want to see what this is about.'

Elaine shrugged. 'As you wish, madame, and what a madame.' She went out and slammed the door just before Eddy and Charles were shown in at the other one.

Lesley welcomed the two men with grace and charm and with the sparkling enquiry of a columnist shining in her eyes.

Eddy introduced Charles as an old friend and once of this parish, now an anthropologist and behaviourist.

'I don't know what a behaviourist is,' Lesley said.

'Nor does he,' said Eddy.

The maid came in with drinks and set the tray on a side table. Lesley went to it. The maid went out.

'Lesley, sweet,' said Eddy putting the letter in front of her, 'why did you write this?'

She looked at it, drew in breath, said, 'Oh!' put a hand to her mouth, then looked at him, turned her head slightly away and burst into tears.

Charles watched curiously. Eddy brought a handkerchief from his pocket and pressed it into her hand.

'Take it before mascara runs like the mud of the Styx.'

She snatched it, stamped on his foot, blew

72

her nose loudly and walked away.

'How did you guess?' she cried.

'You signed it,' Eddy said.

She turned back, eyes wide.

'The style was unmistakable,' Eddy said. 'Why, Lesley? What have you against the widow?'

She sat on the arm of a sofa.

'Do sit down,' she said. 'I can't stand being stood over.'

They sat down.

'Your friend is a criminologist as well, I suppose?' she said ironically.

'We all are, at heart,' said Charles, and beamed.

'I know you're a friend of hers,' said Lesley, 'but what's *your* friend to her?'

'We were all at school together,' said Charles.

'Touching,' said Lesley, calmly. 'Eddy dear, pour out some drinks.' She leaned forward and smiled at Charles. 'Now tell me why you think I would write such a terrible thing about a new widow?'

'You may have wanted to draw attention to a possibility,' Charles said, beaming. 'It is very disturbing if one knows something which was not taken into account in finding out what happened.'

'You think I know something about this man's death?' Lesley looked astonished.

'Surely you would not write if you didn't.'

She did not reply for a moment and to save her inventing anything on the spur of the moment, Eddy handed her a drink. The men sat down and looked at her.

Lesley did not mind being looked at. She loved being looked at, but not in the way the men were looking at her.

'Tell me why you think it's me,' she said, almost cosily.

'The typewriter and your elegant style,' said Eddy.

'I sold that old typewriter,' she said at once. 'I've been given a new one with a golf ball in it and you can change the type when you want.'

'That will be nice—when you get it,' said Eddy. 'Have you ever met Mrs Stong?'

'No. That's why I can't understand what you're talking about.'

'But you knew Adam Stong,' said Eddy, firmly.

'Only very faintly,' she said, looking into the overmantel mirror for a moment. 'He came here once with my daughter. He'd taken her out somewhere and brought her back. He seemed to be drunk and slept it off in a spare room.'

'I'm trying to think why you should have written this, Lesley,' Eddy said, very thoughtfully. 'You don't know her and only saw him once. What gave you the idea?'

'I keep telling you, I didn't have the idea.'

'Perhaps you read the reports of the

inquest?' suggested Charles.

'I saw it of course,' she said. 'I mean it's a dull place. An inquest stands out like a carnival.'

'Perhaps you spoke about it with someone?' Charles said, gently.

'Oh yes, I did, now you come to mention it. Who was it? Grace Wills, I think. At the Country Club. I was there—when was it?— yesterday morning. She was with two others, Mary Ottery and Susan Lilley. They were all talking about it.'

'In what way?' said Eddy.

'Darling,' she said, almost coldly, 'I know you must find out things for your newspaper but you're not a bloody policeman! This sounds like The Inquisition!'

'You said they were talking about it. But an inquest *isn't* a carnival, after all. We do have a few inquests, you know. What was there to talk about in this one?'

'Oh, gossip, you know,' she said, dismissing it with a shrug. 'He was a hound with women. That must have struck your little ear now and again.'

'Yes, but he was dead,' Eddy pointed out. 'Gossip's usually about live people. Yet you say they were all talking about it as if Adam was still a working Casanova.'

'Well, it was something to talk about. I don't know how it came up. I wasn't there when it started!'

'Please don't be angry with us, Lady

75

Hoskins,' Charles said mildly. 'We're only trying to find out where this letter came from.'

'Well, you are friends of hers, so I suppose you are doing a very fine thing,' she said shortly. 'Yes, they were talking about whether the inquest was rigged.'

'You don't know why?'

'I asked why. It all swung round on what sort of man he'd been and what sort of woman she was and they thought she couldn't have gone on taking it lying down. Now you know as much as I do.'

'Then you came home and wrote the letter.'

'No! I sold the bloody typewriter.'

'When? I shall miss it. We had a lot of letters from that old Remington.'

'When did I sell it? Two or three days ago.'

'Oh!' said Charles. 'You wrote the letter before the inquest!'

Lesley looked at the ceiling in a fine show of exasperation.

'I didn't write the bloody letter! I am sick of bloody letters! The way I am just now I won't write another bloody letter as long as I live!'

'Such language, and in front of the vicar!' said Eddy.

'The what?' said Lesley. 'Heavens above! You've been trying to trap me into the confessional!'

As they drove away, Eddy said, 'Well? what do you think?'

'I'm sure she wrote the letter,' said Charles.

76

'And I feel that she knew Adam very well, even that they were very friendly, perhaps much more.

'Prostitutes can suddenly take the most unlikely fancies, or what seem unlikely to outsiders. In this case, the fact that they were each in the business of skinning the opposite sex may have proved a bond between them.'

'And Adam confided in her his fears that he would be bumped off?'

'Yes. And then when it so happened, she wrote the letter but waited till she knew the inquest verdict before she sent it.'

'They must have been unusual friends,' Eddy said. 'To say to a mistress you think your wife is going to have you done in would cure the affair at once. Either way and whatever happened the confidant must lose.'

'She might also find herself in serious trouble,' Charles said.

'Lesley has put herself in such a position,' Eddy said. 'The funny thing is she's been so careless. The old typewriter and no attempt at disguise. She must have known I'd twig as soon as I saw it.'

'Definitely. I go by the burst into tears at the start. I never saw such a phoney job.'

'Then what's her game in doing it like that and then denying it?'

'My dear fellow! You'd better answer that. You know her. I've never seen her before.'

'There have been anonymous letters,' said Philip.

'I have heard,' said Mamsie, putting cheese on a biscuit.

'Where?'

'I found Milly upset this morning. She said she'd heard in the village. Betty Sugden's aunt had one. She works at the Post Office up at the end of the shop counter. You know.'

'What did she do with it?'

'Milly said she burnt it, but she spoke so strongly she might just as well have stuck it up in the window. By mid morning everybody knew.'

'Do you know what it said?'

'Oh, it said I'd had him done in.'

Philip sat back and watched her eat the biscuit and cheese.

'And what are you going to do about it, Mamsie?'

'Sit it through,' she said. 'What else can you do? Tis no good losing your temper against somebody with no name, now, is it?'

'Not really. No. Eddy had a few letters at his office. I expect the police have some, too.'

'Never thought I was so popular,' she said. 'If I did know their names I still wouldn't lose my temper. I'd screw their bloody heads off as quiet as can be. What sort of people are they? What good do they think they're doing for anybody?'

'They're not meaning to do good.'

'Do the letters all say the same thing?'

'In different words, yes.'

'Some one person is behind it, stirring them up,' she said.

'That's possible. Know of anybody?'

'Not unless it's Mr Marks, but he came to say it to my face. No. It would not be he. A woman. Perhaps one of Adam's women. That's possible, but it doesn't sound like a young woman's trick. I reckon you have to be old and bitter over something to start doing that kind of thing.'

'Did you know of Mrs Marks being one of Adam's loves?'

'Yes. That was a good while back. I reckon there's been others since. He couldn't stick. Had to shift all the time.'

'But he stuck with you.'

She laughed ironically.

'For lodgings,' she said. 'But it's funny, as you say, he did stick around. Sometimes he'd look a bit like a dog, I suppose. I've been wondering I wasn't a bit too short with him when he tried to make it up.'

She sighed.

'But you can't keep on, can you? I got taken in too many times, I suppose—Or was it *me*, sometimes? I might have pushed him a bit towards the door—'

'For God's sake, Mamsie, don't start taking the blame for anything. He wasn't worth it.'

'No,' she said, sitting straighter. 'No, he wasn't. But twenty-five years is a long time. Some of it sticks. Most of it doesn't. I'd just like to know this:

'Is it possible that something *did* happen to make him go over Gull Cliff?'

'Anything's possible, Mamsie. There was nothing wrong with the truck mechanically. That was all checked. It was a big fall but it landed on sand. If anything had been wrong to make it go over it would have shown up. You can't hide a thing having been tampered with.'

'Some other way, perhaps?'

'I don't know, and it's no sense in guessing, is there? The police have been through everything. This anonymous letter business can happen anywhere any time. The inquest verdict sparked it all off. Lots of people don't agree with verdicts. They argue about them for days. You must have heard them.'

'You're always arguing in your own favour, Philip,' she said, and smiled. 'Dear Philip. I wish you wouldn't all be trying to help me so much. I can weather it. I always did.'

'The situation is dangerous for you, Mamsie. It may mean trouble if it goes on. The common factor in the majority of the letters seems to be that the writers know Adam didn't go to his death from here.'

She looked watchful.

'How do they know that?'

'He was probably seen that day a long way

80

from the farm here.'

'But he could have come back.'

'That is the point: they seem to know he didn't.'

'But how could they know for certain?'

'They couldn't. But they might start more enquiries to clear up the point and you know he wasn't here. So if there are enquiries they will show that you lied about it. That's a bad start for anything that might follow.'

'Yes. I do see that.'

'And then it will be found you lied to protect Holmes, so what you tried to keep quiet will all come out and then he may be affected, too.'

'I see,' she said, slowly. 'So you want me to do as you tell me?'

'We really believe it's best. It could be a nasty mess if you don't.'

'Somebody is forcing me,' she said, sharply.

'And don't be angry. You'll have to be calm over this and just do what you have to do for the best. Lose your temper and you'll be doing what they want, and that's for the worst.'

'I can understand that, don't fret,' she said.

CHAPTER SIX

1

The afternoon began a game of Find the Lady. Charles went to find Mrs Holmes, perhaps the last person to have seen Adam Stong alive, and certainly the person who had spent much of the last day with him.

She, then, might well have known his intentions for his future, Charles reasoned.

Eddy Worth drove south to the town where Charles Marks claimed to operate his chain of shops. The newspaper office had found no difficulty in tracing the Waga Stores. There were three, and the manager at the first had speedily given Marks' home address.

He gave the impression that he himself would like to contact Mr Marks, but hadn't been able to do so for several days. That was not surprising, he said; Marks often went on holidays unannounced, but this time something had cropped up and he wished to contact the wandering employer.

Eddy came to the detached bungalow about two-thirty. It stood out of the town at the edge of a wood with an older cottage about forty yards away on the left. The road was little more than a quiet lane with a warning notice beyond the Marks' house, 'Ford'.

He stopped the car and walked to the front door of the bungalow. He rang the bell and stood looking round him, and particularly at the nearby cottage. It was quiet. Birds sang in the trees now and again, and he could hear the babbling of the brook the lane went through further on.

There was no answer, as he had expected. He

walked out of the porch and looked at the bungalow, then towards the cottage.

A woman came out of the cottage and looked at him. She then walked to the low hedge as if to look closer.

'They're away, you know,' she said.

He said, 'Oh. Do you know when they might be coming back?'

'I don't exactly. No. He sometimes goes on business like this, but he always leaves me the keys to tidy up and in case of fire or anything.'

'Do you have the keys now?'

'Oh yes.' She reached into the pocket of her jeans and brought out a pair of keys on a ring. She held them up. 'I can let you in if it's important.'

'It is really. It's an insurance survey. If I could just see over. It won't take long.'

Years ago, before the brokers came to town, The Post had taken on the agency for an insurance company, and affection, long contact and generous terms had made the paper hold on. So that he did not lie that much.

'I'll come round,' she said.

'You're very kind. It would save me a lot.'

She came round. She was plump and her jersey and tight jeans strained to contain her advantages. She smiled cheerfully.

'There's been one or two,' she said, 'but they didn't need for to go in. The Electricity and that. They just estimate it, so they owe you something when you pay.'

She sorted the two keys when they came to the door.

'I never do remember which one's which, they both look the same, you see. I married a twin brother, and it's the same with them, too. Sometimes you start saying something and it's the wrong one. It makes you very careful. Ah! that's the one.'

She opened the door and led the way in.

'Works on the farms. My husband. Mends the tractors and combines. Makes him hungry, I can tell you.'

Eddy looked round. It was well furnished in a modern, copied-out-of-glossy style, and tidy, as if nobody had lived there for some time.

It was easy to see all this for all the doors were open on to the square hall.

'When did they go?' he said.

'They? Tisn't they. She haven't been here some time now. Could be on for a year. She's come here now and again, that's all, mostly when he isn't here, either.'

She looked at him to see if he understood her.

'Separated, are they?' he said. He took out a notebook and seemed to be taking notes of the structure and decorations.

'I don't know what they are. Tis a funny sort of how-de-do, to me. Fellers. She always seemed to have fellers. What he did I don't know because I never seen him with a woman. Praps that's why he goes away often. Though

84

he does go for business,' she added, as an afterthought.

He grinned. He thought if he played the right part he could pick up a lot as they walked around the rooms.

'So they don't get on together,' he said.

'I don't know how to put it. She used to come back and they'd get on all right, from the outside, I mean, then she'd start coming back with some feller or the other—of course he was out a lot anyway for business—and then she'd go off and you wouldn't see her for quite some time. It was like I say, weird. For married people, I mean.'

She frowned.

'Funny thing, they used to fight like mad, too. It didn't seem to go with the rest, somehow.'

'You talk as if they'd gone.'

'Well, I think she's gone. Haven't seen her some time. If she don't come back I think he'll sell this place. It's a bit big for one.'

'Do you think he might sell his business?' he said, still jotting things down.

'Oh no, he won't leave here, just get something smaller, a flat or that. He's said that sometimes.'

'He's mentioned it to you?'

'Oh yes. He comes in for tea when he's alone and so'm I. You get miserable on your own. I do. Like somebody to talk to. Like a man best. Women's all gossip. It's all going over and over what you heard already.'

'You sound a little bit naughty to me,' he said, and smiled.

'With Mr Marks, you mean?' She winked. 'Oh well. What the eye don't see the heart don't grieve over.'

They went into another room.

'I was surprised, really,' she said. 'They say people who have to do with all this porn and sex stuff aren't sexy.'

'Is that what he sells?'

'No, not just that. It's a health food and medicine shop in front and you go into the back for the other.'

'Oh, I see. I thought they were general stores.'

'Well, they're pretty general,' she said. 'There's a lot of them about now, he says. It's just a trade like anything—' She broke off and stared out of the window. 'Bless me! There she is! Coming right up to the front door calm as you like.'

'Mrs Marks?' he said quickly.

'Yes. And done up to the nines, but no feller.' She glanced at him. 'Well, I can leave her to do you, I suppose.' She smiled.

2

Mrs Marks was beautiful in a rather well-finished way. Her make-up revealed careful attention to detail and effect. Her eyes were grey, sometimes like ice, then suddenly lighting up with a gleam of unsuspected humour.

He reckoned she was around forty.

'I wouldn't know what my husband has been talking about,' she said. 'We don't meet unless it's very urgent business.'

'It was just that he mentioned insurance and he was interested in our shell cover. Building, that is, not the contents.'

'I didn't know you made a survey,' she said, evenly.

'We are sometimes advised to do it.'

'Well, it's nice to see someone, anyway.' She tossed her gloves on to a coffee table. 'I hate coming back to an empty house. I can't make tea. I'll get some drinks.'

He did not normally drink liquor between half-two and half-four in the daytime, but he was a journalist and ready to suffer in the cause of truth.

'You come from Up There, do you?' she said. 'I have a sort of brother-in-law up there. Adam Stong. Have you come across him?'

He said, 'I read the report of his inquest yesterday.'

He meant maximum shock to her, but she turned away to pour out drinks and he could not see her face.

'He's dead, do you mean?'

'Yes. He had a car accident. I'm sorry. I thought you might know.'

She turned and looked at him.

'Now why on earth should you think I

know?'

'Your husband was up there. I suppose that's why.'

'I said I don't see my husband over trivial affairs.'

'I'm sorry. I just thought you might have heard.'

She turned back to the table, took up two drinks, turned back and handed him one.

'We have met before,' she said.

'We have? I must have had my eyes shut.'

'Your eyes were on the coroner and the witnesses as they came in. You were in the press enclosure. You were reporting the proceedings.'

'I am on the Post. Yes. We have an agency for the Moonstar Insurance Company.'

'Well, that's your story,' she said. 'Now here's mine. You came here because you think my husband killed Adam Stong.'

'If I did, I would have gone to the police. I know every member of the force.'

'They'd hardly be impressed. The verdict of the inquest being against you.'

'I said I know them all. They would have talked to me about it and kept it in mind.'

She sat down gracefully.

'I thought the wife was very well treated by the coroner,' she said.

'He's usually considerate to new widows.'

'I meant that he took her word for everything.'

88

'She didn't know anything, except her husband drank too much before it.'

'Yes. She did say that. It struck me she was glad to be rid of him.'

'He was your brother-in-law, you say. Didn't you ever meet his wife?'

'Yes. We didn't hit it off. That is, we hit, but it was a different kind of hitting.'

'So you met only once?'

'No. But after the first time we talked from a safe distance.'

'You seem to do the same thing with your husband.'

'May I tell you a secret, Mr Worth?'

'Naturally, I'd like it.'

'I don't like people.'

'I don't like *all* of them. Some I dislike. Some I hate. Usually the ones I hate are those who insist on shoving themselves under my nose and talking about what most affects me. Most of them I've never met.'

'Now that we've introduced ourselves to our nasty bits, let us get down to business. Do you think my husband had something to do with Adam's death?'

'I don't know. He said you'd had an affair with Adam, if that's what you want to know.'

'I had several with Adam. He was that kind of man. You'd have him, then he'd drive you crazy and you'd show him the door. Then after a while you wanted to see him again, so off you went again on the same roundabout, with the

89

same half ending.'

'If you were a woman,' he suggested.

'My dear man—men couldn't stick him. If Adam wanted something from a man he'd steal his wife and get it that way.'

'By blackmail, do you mean?'

She shrugged.

'That's only one way. He had plenty of other ways. He would get round the wife to ask the husband for what he wanted. He was an unprincipled sod.'

'Yet you got on with him?'

'I'm pretty unprincipled myself. He had immense charm which he could turn on and off when wanted, like a television, loud, bright or any degree of either that would suit the woman victim.'

'You are very frank.'

'I bare my breast when it suits my purpose.'

'And what purpose have you conceived for me?'

She sat back.

'Do you know,' she said, 'I think you and I could get on together. A couple of cynical sophisticates; that is, soaked in sin.'

'Not complimentary.'

'Look here, why should I be? You come here on a press snoop, lie to my neighbour and watchdog, and try the same lie on me but fail, then punt around in a cosy chat making mental notes of what I say so you can computer it out later. Taking all that into account, what do you

90

call yourself?'

'An unfair question. I wouldn't think of it as you do.'

'Do you know what I am?'

'The wife of Charles Marks, former mistress and outside relative of Adam Stong. That's all.'

'I didn't say who. I said what.'

'As a profession, do you mean?'

'Yes.'

'The oldest.'

She laughed.

'Was that a guess? Anyhow, it's right. I am a whore, and I have a business interest up in your part of the country.'

'Lady Lesley Hoskins,' he said.

'Oh, you know?'

'A lot of people know. That's what business is—getting known to start with.'

He stacked a thought into his head for future reference. The anonymous letter had come from Lesley, and she had been very friendly with Adam, and now there was a connection directly to Mark's wife.

'I was a nympho,' she said. 'Still am, for that matter, but decided not to be so generous. We run girls. They make a lot of money. So do we.'

'Lady Lesley's place must be very expensive,' he said, drily.

'It costs a bomb. We make a bomb. Newton's law is satisfied.'

'You're in partnership?'

91

'That's it. People think it must be illegal. It isn't. We don't call it a brothel. It's a business agency.'

He sipped his drink and watched her.

'A gilt vice shop,' he said. 'And what did Adam have to do with all this?'

'I can't say. Do you smoke? No?' She took a cigarette from a box. 'Well now you know everything. My husband runs a few porn shops but they don't do very well. They're supposed to help the weak, but the weak help themselves too much.'

'I thought he did well from them.'

'He doesn't care about them. To tell the truth, he doesn't like the idea. Neither do I. He thought they would make money. He'll go into anything for money. That's how Adam diddled him. He played on Charles's greed, and won.'

'You mean Adam suggested he buy these shops?'

'Yes. It was a few years ago. He said he could get them cheap—the shops, that is. They did make a lot at one time, but the whole thing's gone out of fashion. People are turning their backs on that sort of thing, thank the lord.'

'You treat everything as a business?'

'Not everything. I have my feelings. The trouble is whenever I go by my feelings I get done in the eye, so I don't use them too much.'

'It must be a cold sort of life for you.'

'All right. I'm a bitch. What do you call yourself—ferret?'

She laughed.

'It's been an interesting chat—' he said.

'It will go on being interesting,' she said.

'I don't quite get you.'

'You're not going,' she said.

'But I am.'

'I said you're not. You stay and keep me company. I am quite able to entertain you.'

'I don't doubt that,' he said.

'You have no wife to run home to, so why the rush?'

'How do you know I've no wife?'

'When you play detective, my boy, you want to make sure at the start that you're not setting yourself against a detective.'

He offered his glass.

'I'll have another drink.' he said.

'Very wise,' she said. 'I don't want to be melodramatic, but you know, in my industry, we are obliged to carry insurance.'

'Protectors?' he said. 'Yes, I do know. No, I don't want to disagree with one over your welfare. I don't wonder your husband doesn't contact you much. He might be done over as well, I suppose?'

'You mistake me. I am not a vicious bitch. I want a peaceful life. I don't want fights physical or in the press.'

'I see. But I'm not here for the press. I came to help Adam's widow. She is in trouble.'

'Somebody has found her out?'

'No. Somebody is trying to stick one on her.

Anonymous letters.'

'That's filthy. That's about the only thing we'll agree on about her, I think. But how on earth can you help her by snooping around here?'

'I wasn't sure, but now I have a lead. You see, the leading poison letter was written by your partner, Lady Lesley Hoskins.'

She sat up straight in astonishment.

'What? Are you sure?'

'Yes. I know her very well. I called on her this morning. She admitted it. She also sent one to the police,' he added in a generous lie.

She stubbed her cigarette out and stood up.

'Right. I won't keep you here. You can go back to see Lesley, and I'm coming with you.'

Sometimes the lie is worth more than the truth, he thought.

3

The Reverend Charles was lucky to find Mrs Holmes alone. In fact, she was alone a lot. To eke out an income from a failing small farm, Holmes was a traveller from an outside firm covering a fair-sized area.

Mrs Holmes was a big, loose woman, not pretty but attractive in a careless, easy way. It was mid-afternoon when he got there and she was wearing sandals, a silk dressing gown and, it appeared, little else.

'I wonder if you could help me?' he said, in his most charming manner.

94

'Any way,' she said, and smiled.

Though inclined to lie, Charles felt somehow it would be best to be forthright. She did not look a sort of woman who could be easily lied to. He noticed she had a funny way of half turning her head and looking at him as if some sort of witch's glance enabled her to look through his face right into what he was thinking.

He felt an odd desire to giggle at the idea.

'It's about Mrs Stong,' he said frankly.

'What's the matter with her?' Her glance was less warm at the mention of the name. She turned away. 'Come and sit down and tell me. I'll get a cup of tea.'

They went through into a big kitchen. He sat down at the scrubbed table. She went to put a kettle on. He realised it would be difficult to talk if she moved about, and clearly, she realised it would be easier for her.

'You know that the inquest found accidental death,' he said. 'And so all should be over and done with. But a number of anonymous letters have been sent, suggesting that she got someone to kill her husband.'

She put on a kettle then stopped still, looking out of the window.

'She told a story to protect my Jim,' she said.

'Yes, I know that. But it wasn't thought that anybody else knew it. I am a very old friend of hers and—'

'My dear Charlie, I remember you as a big

95

boy when I was about five. You smacked my bum once for kicking a spoke out of your bike wheel. That's why I remember you.'

She laughed, and so did he.

'I'm sorry I didn't recognise you,' he said.

'We moved off to Barnstaple. Came back here when I married Jim.' She looked out of the window again. 'What are these letters about?'

'They're really about the time before he went over the cliff,' he said. 'They said he didn't go from home. Mamsie knew he was here but saw no sense in dragging others into the wretched business when his death had been an accident.'

'Mamsie is big all ways,' she said. 'But she's been too bloody generous in thinking I was after her husband. I wouldn't have touched that little bastard with the dirty end of a barge pole.'

Charles was surprised.

'But he was here?' he said.

'Oh yes, he was here,' she said. She poured water into the pot and clapped the lid on. 'He was here and he was pissed. I don't mean that he was tight, I don't mean that he was drunk, I mean he was so far gone he didn't know what the hell he was doing.

'He went on and on drinking. He was here all day, bottle after bottle. I think he had four. At one time I thought he was trying to kill himself. It can be done, I've heard.'

'But why did he come here to do it?' he said.

96

She looked out of the window again.

'I won't tell that,' she said.

CHAPTER SEVEN

1

When Eddy drove up to Lady Lesley's fine house, Mrs Marks changed her mind.

'I'll fight her alone over this,' she said. 'No doubt we shall meet again.'

'I think no doubt at all,' he said.

When she had got out he drove away back to his office. He was only a little surprised to find Jamey and Philip talking together, waiting for him.

He closed the door.

'Anything?' Philip said briefly.

'Plenty.'

He told of Mrs Marks and her ladyship.

'Marks,' said Jamey, scratching his nose. 'That feller came and asked me questions about Adam—and Mamsie of course.'

'There is something too bloody open about Marks making himself known round here,' Eddy said. 'Does that strike you?'

'It strikes me,' Philip agreed.

'Well, I only saw him that one time,' Jamey said. 'But he didn't make a secret of his name nor what he'd come for.' He frowned. 'I always thought brothels were illegal.'

'Only if the girls live in,' said Philip. 'Curious

laws we have, thank the lord.'

'The point I was turning over in my nut is that such industries can attract heavy mobs. Mrs Marks talked of her protectors, for instance,' Eddy said. 'Now, if there were heavies around and Adam got on the wrong side of them, it might have been his fatal mistake.'

'A good headline,' said Philip, 'but it doesn't help at all. What we want to know is the sequence of events the day he died. We know about Jessie Holmes but nothing else.'

'Mrs Marks and her partner know a lot—if not all,' Eddy said. 'But in their different ways they're both good clams. I'm puzzled as to Mrs Marks' panic when I said Lesley had sent the letter, after Lesley seemed to go out of her way to make sure we *knew* she'd sent it.'

'I don't see this is to do with their business,' said Jamey. 'Or do you mean Adam had to do with the brothel industry?'

'That, and his pushing Marks into the porn business seems to indicate that he was out for money, one way or the other.'

'Which brings us back to the point; is there any money of Adam's lying about, and if there is, where is it?' Philip said. 'As one doesn't buy shares in bordellos it's more likely he acted as an agent of some kind.'

'A pimp,' said Jamey. 'In history, you know they made lots of money. Casanova, you see, worn out before he was forty, became a successful agent.'

'I didn't know that,' said Philip, and looked at Eddy. 'Are we to think of Adam as wildly successful so as to make his death worth while?'

The Reverend Charles was announced, and came in to tell of Jessie Holmes.

'And she won't say why he was in that state?' Philip said.

'He could drink plenty,' Eddy said. 'Two or three bottles maybe. He was well saturated all the time of late years. It didn't affect his head like it does most.'

'But she said he was very badly drunk,' Charles said. 'And he had told her why, so it must have been something to do with her. She seemed a very normal person, if careless.'

'I suppose he wasn't blackmailing?' Jamey said. 'I mean, by all account he seems to have done most other things that were disreputable.'

Charles looked out of the window at the evening sun.

'I think Mamsie does know everything that happened that day,' he said.

'She said she didn't,' said Philip, curiously.

'Mamsie was always very good at saying she didn't,' said Charles, 'when very often, she did.'

'So far,' Philip said, 'we have sorted out a few people who were concerned with Adam and might have seen him that day. I have a feeling—no special reason for it—that there is one more person we haven't contacted because we don't know about them.'

'Supposing that one is Mamsie?' said Charles, turning back.

'She has said she didn't see him after he took the Land-Rover to have it serviced,' Eddy said.

'He went to Mrs Holmes at about three in the afternoon,' said Charles, 'and Holmes came back and found him about ten.'

Philip looked up sharply.

'It must have been later than that?' he said. 'What time was the accident?'

'About quarter to twelve, estimated.'

'If she's right, then he probably saw somebody after he left her,' Eddy said.

'Or he might have gone back to the farm,' Charles said.

'What are you doing—trying to prove her guilty?' said Jamey, surprised.

'Yes,' Charles said. 'That is the purpose of the letters and the gossip. If we can find a point of view that might agree with theirs, then between theirs and ours we might find the truth.'

'I don't know that I like that,' Jamey said. 'I mean, in the first place why make a murder out of an accidental death? Are the police going to take any notice of the anonymous letters? They say they don't.'

'It depends how many and how long they go on,' said Eddy. 'If they become persistent, the police might look into who's sending them.

From that, anything could happen.'

'The real danger is that nothing will be done about them,' Charles said. 'Rumour grows. In this case there is something to start it, and because of that I think it'll go on, and get worse and Mamsie will have to bear it for the rest of her life here. Gossip is one thing about death that doesn't die with it.'

'You must have an immoral parish,' Jamey said, and laughed. 'But tis right. Some of the things I hear about the Sorely Missed and Dearly Beloved almost make me shake when I cut the names in my headstones.'

'I often wonder why there was no God of Humbug amongst the legendary gods,' said Eddy. 'He could have outweighed Titan.'

'Charles,' Philip said, 'what are you after? What do you mean we should do?'

'We should all go and question Mamsie,' said Charles quietly.

'She will feel assailed,' said Jamey.

'In which case she'll assail right back,' said Eddy. 'And she's more likely to let slip anything she does know if she really lets fly.'

2

At six twenty that evening Lady Lesley Hoskins called unexpectedly at the farm. She and Mamsie had known each other a few years before when both were elected to the committee of the same charitable organisation.

Lady Lesley had been asked to resign.

101

Mamsie had opposed the motion on the grounds that what she was doing for the organisation was entirely for good and that was all that mattered. The other members had decided they would not sit with an uncommon prostitute, though several tried to reverse the decision later, when they heard she had plenty of money.

Mamsie looked askance when she came into the farmhouse.

'Haven't seen you for quite five years,' she said.

'I don't remember years,' said Lesley. 'They kill my youthful charm. I wouldn't have come now but an unfortunate event draws us together in common suffering.'

'I don't intend to do any suffering,' said Mamsie. 'You can have my half.'

'You've guessed what the sad event is?' Lesley looked surprised.

'Adam, I suppose.'

'Well, Adam eventually, yes. Or I should say Adam incidentally. It's about some anonymous letters.'

'I've heard. But how do they affect you?'

'Like this. Today Mr Worth, the newspaper man, called on me with a friend, some kind of parson, I gather. They accused me of writing one.'

'Did you?'

'Yes. I wanted him to come, you see, but having the other man with him spoilt it.'

102

'All right. Why did you write it? Stupidity?'

'Cunning. I wanted to see him about the whole thing but I know if I write or phone everybody in the office would know, and they all know me.'

'What do you care if they know you?'

'I'm thinking of Eddy.'

She smiled. Mamsie smiled back, then laughed.

'Get on. I don't understand about the letter.'

'I didn't understand myself until he came and then I began to get the drift that it might affect me—the death, I mean.'

'Go on.'

'I didn't know about the fact that Adam might have called on people before it happened. That rather altered it for me.'

'He called on you?'

'Yes. He came, I suppose it was about eleven. He was stinking. You know he could take a lot before he got blind-oh, but that night he was *stupid*. I thought he might have gone a bit mad, actually.'

'Go on. Why?'

'He bellowed about being no good, wicked to you—'

'To *me*?'

'Yes. No doubt about it, either. He went on and on, and I said, "If you feel like that about it you'd better go right back and tell her." That seemed the only thing, as far as I could see. I mean, plenty come and cry about being ill-

103

treated and misunderstood and the rest of the old baloney, but Adam's angle was new to me.'

'Oh,' said Mamsie slowly, 'I see what you mean.'

'Yes. He said he'd go right back and left.'

'He didn't come here.'

'He had time. He left at twenty past eleven. I looked at the clock because I was very anxious he should get out of the way and not smash up right outside. He went quietly.'

'You kept very quiet too.'

'I don't want any mention at inquests, dear,' Lesley said. 'All that sort of thing is very bad for me. We are an exclusive establishment.'

'I didn't know he went to you, but there's a lot I don't know.'

'He didn't come for relief in the physical sense. He came—well, to chat. He was always mad to get a girl to chat to.'

'He paid for that?' Mamsie smiled wryly.

'He didn't pay at all—' Lesley broke off, then changed the subject. 'You see, I thought you ought to know in case—'

'Why didn't he pay? It was girls' time, wasn't it? And that's what men pay for isn't it?'

Lesley sighed and then shrugged.

'One time,' she said, 'he lent us a bomb of money to help us get the house there. I suppose you didn't know? He wanted it kept quiet. He was insistent about that. I shouldn't have said, but I slipped up over not paying later on.'

'How much did he lend?'

'You needn't worry about that. He was very careful to say it wasn't anything to do with you or the farm—'

'How much?'

'Well, it wasn't only the house, but we had to furnish it quite specially, you know—' She sighed again. 'Twenty thousand.'

Mamsie just nodded.

'And you said you paid him back, did you?'

'Every cent, in cash.'

'Cash? Loose money?'

'He insisted. No records. That was his condition. He lent cash, we paid back cash.'

'With interest?'

'Of course. And bonuses.'

'How long ago did you pay him back?'

'About two years.'

'I never knew he had any money,' Mamsie said.

'He said it was quite separate from the farm,' Lesley hastened to assure her. 'His business was separate. He always made that clear.'

'I didn't know he had a business,' Mamsie said.

She was so quiet and calm, Lesley began to feel tense, uneasy.

'I don't know that it was a business,' she said quickly. 'It might have been—anything.'

'In cash?'

'Well no, but it could have been gambling. Anything like that. Or he could have borrowed it himself, you know, and kept the interest—'

Mamsie just shook her head, then watched the visitor for a moment.

'You didn't mean to tell me. It was just the way the questions fell in place,' Mamsie said. 'So leave that. But what are you frightened of about what he did that night?'

'Well, you see when the rumour was about you'd got somebody to kill him, I didn't see the angle till a couple of hours ago.'

'What angle?'

'Well—the angle that I might have been the one you chose.'

Mamsie was silent for some time.

'Say something!' Lesley said.

'I'm trying to think what anybody else might say to it,' Mamsie said. 'But you paid back the money, so you should be clear. Or did he ask for it suddenly?'

'Yes. We had to borrow to pay him. We didn't expect it.'

'Have you paid it back? To the other people, I mean.'

'No. Not all of it.'

'Are they asking?'

'Yes. That doesn't help my angle, does it?'

'What made you think of it, only an hour or two ago?'

'One of our girls. She said if anyone had knocked him off it would surely be a woman. I said how could the woman make that accident? and she said easy, just pass him on that narrow road and then force him over so he went

106

through the fence.

'She knew that he'd been drunk and said he could tread the wrong pedal easily, the state he was in.'

'What made her think of that?' Mamsie said.

'Well, they all knew him so well and there is this gossip around. It's natural they should have guessing games about it.'

'Did you leave the house after he'd gone?'

'I was waiting for that. Yes.' She laughed briefly. 'A dead loser, this one. I wanted air. I have a dog. I decided to go out up to the cliffs and walk him there.'

She sat back, slightly relaxed. 'So you see why I thought I'd tell you.'

Mamsie shook her head.

'I never thought anything so simple could come to such a mess.'

'No. It was a mess before. That's why it happened, I think.'

3

Harry did not concern himself overmuch with human problems. He had found that if he did he got worried and then depressed and then went to the drink, so he preferred his animals.

The thought of the horses coming down filled his mind more than the gossip which was scaring Milly. That evening, before going home, he remembered some old harness which was still hanging somewhere in the tithe barn.

It was a fine barn, admired by visitors, a

preserved building, protected by law, of granite, wood and thatch. Once the tithe collector had slept inside and his little room by the big main door was still there, and Harry thought the harness pieces were somewhere in that room.

The room was not used except to heap in unwanted small bits and pieces that might someday be useful. It was a right muddle of oddments.

He started to hunt amongst the stuff, stopping to ponder some fearful veterinary instrument from the days when the vet hadn't been too handy. He liked the surgical bits which made him imagine fearful deeds.

Poking around amongst some old leathers, long past being brought back to use, he found part of the chains of a harness, dusty and rusty, but a good shaking in a sack of sand would clean it up special.

It was when he tried to free the chain from something catching it on the floor that the trapdoor came up.

The sudden rising of the flap with a sad groan made him start. He muttered something to soothe his nerves then peered into the gap in the floor.

There were ammunition boxes, the old big ones that held a hundred or two shotgun cartridges, piled down there and they didn't look that dirty or dusty or stained.

'Bloody Irish!' he said. 'A dump!'

He took up a box. It wasn't very heavy, as it should have been. He shook it, but it didn't rattle even a little.

He took the lid off. It was stuffed full of five pound notes. A man of quiet consideration, he cleared a space on the old collector's table with an elbow and put the box down. He then took out several more boxes and put them on the table, then he sat down after lifting his newly discovered harness from the seat of the chair.

Box by box he removed the lids until he saw seven boxes all full of paper money, some fives, some tens, some twenties all mixed up together.

He sat back and stared at the boxes of money.

'Money,' he muttered. 'Undreds of thousands of bloody fine money! Money! All money! Stone the bloody crows! It makes me cry, that does.'

He took some notes out of a box and made sure it was money all the way down, clean notes, dirty notes, dog-eared notes, notes stuck up with Sellotape, stamp paper and some even a bit burnt.

'Makes yer cry, that does,' he said. 'Strikes right at the 'eart.' Again he sat back. He wiped his brow with his hat screwed up in his fist. 'What to do?'

He sat for some time trying to answer his own question, then he got up, put the lids on and stacked all the boxes back under the floor. He lowered the trap into place and put some old leathers on top.

Native cunning was not stunned by his discovery. He took up the harness chains he had found and carried them out into the evening sun.

He slung the chains over his shoulder and then saw the man standing by the five bar gate, watching him. The man who had been there before, staring round the place, nosing.

Harry turned and went to his old van parked round by the fuel sheds. He heaved the chains in through the open back doors then shut them and looked along towards the gate again.

The man was standing just back from the gate, but he wasn't watching the barn then.

He was watching Harry.

Harry went round the other side of the van and got into the driver's seat, slamming the door with a clang.

'He couldn't know,' Harry said, uneasily. 'That winder was all dirt. He couldn't have seen through.'

He started up and drove to the gate, got out and opened it.

'I'm on the look-out for old harness,' Marks said. 'I pay a good price.'

'These are for horses,' said Harry, without looking at the buyer. He turned to go back to the van.

'Do you work horses on this farm?' Marks said.

'We're having more, to work,' Harry said.

'We only got one now, big bugger, she is, and kick the edd off any nosey sods asking questions and nosing round.'

The visitor shrugged.

Harry got back in the van, drove through, got out, shut the gate, got back in, clanged the door shut then looked out of the window at the motionless watcher.

'What's the matter with you, matey?' he said. 'Got struck, ave you?'

'I'm waiting to see Mrs Stong,' Marks said. 'She is busy at the moment.'

Harry considered starting the van, but then decided he didn't want to go and leave the man standing around, because of what he might have seen.

Harry got out, muttering something bad-temperedly about having forgotten 'the bit'.

He clambered over the gate and tramped back into the barn again. Once inside he got well back into the shadows and watched the man.

He kicked things about to make a noise of searching, but the man seemed to lose interest and turned to look at the farmhouse.

Pushing and kicking loose straw amid the bales shifted one pack slightly, so he kicked in between that loose one and the next and his foot jolted hard so it hurt his toe even through the big boot.

He looked out at the man, but Marks was still watching the farmhouse.

111

Harry's mind was fixed on boxes of money and, very quickly, he bent and peered into the gap between the bales. It was dark in there, so he put his hand in down towards the floor, searching for boxes.

His hand touched straw or frayed string or something, and he felt past it, turning his head to see the man suddenly turn and walk away into the lane.

Harry heaved the loose bale aside so a little daylight got into the gap.

It was hairs he had hold of, and they were, as usual, attached to a head.

CHAPTER EIGHT

1

'What you doing, Harry?'

Harry froze. For a second or more he could not move at all but just stood by the gap between the hay bales, even his heart stopped by the sound of Millie's voice behind him.

Heat flooded back into him.

'Just seeing all's right,' he said, half choking.

He did not know what to do. He had found a dead woman, but the feeling of guilt he already had over the hidden money extended somehow to the murder as well.

'You look all funny,' she said, coming closer. 'What's the matter?'

112

'Nothing,' he croaked. 'Just clearing up a few things.'

Some sense returned and he began to wonder why he was keeping the murder hidden, but he felt that, as he had started doing it, he had better go on and say nothing to anybody. Let them find it. That was best.

If the police came and started searching, they would find all that money, for sure. He had not thought out what he might do with it, and how he might get away with keeping it; he had not imagined much but the feeling that for the moment he felt rich. There was no sense to that, either, but he was confused and frightened by the rapid turn of events and in a near panic the money and the murder seemed certain to be part of the same thing.

'Give us a kiss, then,' she said.

'All right,' he said, and grabbed her tight.

'Gosh! What's the matter?' she gasped, and tried to push him away. 'Let go, Harry!'

Harry let go. She stood staring keenly at him. The evening light was shining directly on his features and she could read fear in his face.

'What is it, Harry?' She took his arm and shook it. 'What's happened?'

'I—' Harry swallowed hard. 'I found—somebody. The minute you come in, I found it. By the bale there. Don't touch nothing—not yet—'

Millie pulled him slightly aside and looked down between the bales. She stopped still.

'My God!' she said, and closed her eyes.

'Millie!' Mamsie called from out in the yard. 'Millie?'

Millie let out part of a small scream then clapped her hand over her mouth too late. Mamsie came to the barn door and looked in.

'Missus—' Harry said, and swallowed again, '—tis something bad. Here. Bad.'

Mamsie came into the barn, drawn by the dramatic appearance of the two facing her. A few paces behind her, languidly curious, came Lady Lesley, a connoisseur of short screams.

Mamsie went to the bale where Harry pointed. Lesley stood in the doorway, and watched with increasing curiosity.

'Somebody dead?' she said, airily.

'Yes,' Mamsie said. 'Murdered, by the look of it.'

Lesley said something they did not hear then aloud, 'Who?'

'I don't know for sure,' Mamsie said. 'A woman.'

She looked at Milly. 'Have you seen her before?'

Milly just hissed and shook her head.

'Not round here,' Harry said. 'Stranger to me, she is.'

'Are you serious?' Lesley said, walking in quickly.

'Yes,' Mamsie said. 'Look. Do you know her?'

Lesley stopped and looked. She gave an

114

exclamation of great strength.

'You know her!' Mamsie said.

'Yes. A partner in my business. That is Mrs Marks.'

'Marks!' Harry said. 'Damn me! He was here hanging round not five minutes back!'

'Are you sure?' Mamsie said, uneasily.

'For sure I spoke with him. He said as he wanted to buy harness off me.'

There was a silence. Harry's jaws were moving without any effect, and sweat on his face glistened in the evening light. Millie watched him anxiously, as if his very look made her nervous that he might have had something to do with it.

A car pulled up by the gate. Harry started. The three women looked round.

'Eddy,' Mamsie said, going to the door. 'He'll know what to do.'

'But surely we know what to do,' said Lesley, in an odd tone. 'One is supposed to call the police. Not that I am in favour of these people asking questions and giving one the wrong publicity.'

Mamsie went out. In a moment she came back with Eddy. He had a look. The witnesses left him plenty of room.

He looked closer. He stood back.

'I brought her up here,' he said, huskily. 'I dropped her at your place, Lesley. About half four.'

'I didn't see her,' Lesley said. 'I didn't know

she was up here. She said she was going abroad. That was yesterday.'

'Shouldn't we better get the police now?' said Millie suddenly.

'Why did she rush back up?' Lesley said. 'Did she say?'

'She wanted to see you on a business matter,' Eddy said.

'But I cleared everything with her last night!' Lesley sounded angry. 'She said she was going for two or three months. There wasn't anything she had to see me about.'

'She said something about a letter, that was all,' Eddy said. 'It seemed pretty urgent to me.'

'I'll phone the police,' Mamsie said, turning to the door.

'No point in us standing here,' Eddy said. 'Nobody'll touch anything. Let's all go inside.'

'I'll wait by the door if you like,' Harry said.

'You can watch from the kitchen window,' Millie said, quick with relief. 'I'll make tea.'

'Yes, do that,' Mamsie said.

2

'Don't ring. Not yet,' Eddy said.

Mamsie stopped by the phone and looked at him. Lesley turned away, hiding a look of faint relief.

'But it's right to call them,' Mamsie said, staring.

'We'll call them,' said Eddy. 'But there's no law that says you must do it at once. See if you

116

can get hold of Philip.'

'What are you up to?' Mamsie said.

'There are a number of things which are very suspicious in this. First, it's been done in your barn. That seems to me to suggest it's meant to hang on you. Why pick the barn? It isn't deserted. It must have been a risk, knowing people are about all the time.'

'Marks was here,' said Mamsie.

'Surely that lets him out? There are plenty of more secluded places he could have chosen for such a job. Besides, if he had done it in a temper he would hardly have stood around just after, offering to buy harness.'

'He wouldn't kill her,' said Lesley, turning. 'They were not concerned with each other's lives. In practice they'd broken up years ago. There wouldn't be any point in it.'

'She was your sister-in-law, Mamsie,' Eddy said.

'I haven't seen her for years. In fact I wasn't sure it was her just now. Not till it was said.'

'Nobody saw her come?' Eddy said.

'No. I can't think how she came to be there.'

'She never went anywhere without a reason,' said Lesley, in a hard tone of voice. 'A more practical, cold hearted bitch you never came across. She came here for something, that's certain.'

'And I seem to be the only person who knew she was in the district,' Eddy said.

'I'll ring Philip,' Mamsie said. 'He'll know

what's best.'

She could not get Philip at his home, but Charles was there, trying to find Philip, so Mamsie asked Charles to come out.

'Oh lord,' Eddy said. 'I can't see him holding back once he knows.' He marched up and down the room, then stopped. 'Well, we'll wait for him, anyway.'

'I don't know why you're waiting,' said Mamsie, evenly. 'Why not tell me?'

'He thinks it best,' said Lesley. 'I think it best. Sophisticated business people consider matters before they bring in the heavy feet to ruin the merchandise.'

'The police will have to come,' said Mamsie, more evenly.

'Of course,' said Eddy, edgily. 'We all know that. I just think it would be best if we sorted our heads out first. What you have to bear in mind is, that though we may all be innocent, the police may not think so, and that could be very damaging. That is why I want to see Philip first.'

Mamsie knew what he meant. With the air already full of rumour and anonymous letters, a death in her own barn would cause very much more trouble than just wild suggestion. It would seem to justify a more solid investigation into the first rumour.

She had a mind to bring it out quickly and get it over with. One fight and finish, not skulking about round under the hedges hoping it would all go away.

She thought for a moment of her 'new life' of yesterday, so swiftly swallowed up by Adam, as if he had come back to life, worse than before.

'What's Philip going to do?' Mamsie said. 'What can he do except stand by and see they don't trick us into saying something we shouldn't?'

'How long since you've seen her? Mrs Marks?'

'Years. I forget how many. There's an awful lot of blood—I didn't recognise her at once.'

'Do you know of anyone who might have wanted to kill her?' Eddy said, turning to Lesley.

She shook her head.

'I tell you, she was a cold lot, a calculating bitch. She didn't engender passion that could end up in this. No. She was hit with a chopper, wasn't she?'

'Something like that,' Eddy said.

Charles arrived. Eddy told him what they had found, and took him out and let him see. They were gone some minutes.

'You'll have a job, getting out of this,' Lesley said, and shrugged. 'You do realise that?'

'If it was meant to fix me, it won't,' said Mamsie. 'Once they find out why she came. That's the thing. Why did she come? She has never been here. Never at all.'

'Funny, for a relative, isn't it?'

'She was having my husband, right from the start. I said if she came near me or the farm I would—'

Lesley watched and waited, but she did not go on.

'You would have done,' she said. 'And they'll say you have.'

'But he's dead now,' Mamsie said. 'So why would I?'

'I don't know,' Lesley said. 'Adam certainly made trouble.'

'Perhaps she was going to meet someone here,' Mamsie said. 'But it would be funny using someone else's barn for a meeting. A barn right next to the house, almost.'

'That's not the only entrance, is it? That huge one?'

'No, there's two small doors, but the big doors are never shut and people go about the yard all day, and the dogs—funny they didn't kick up. They must have been out across the fields somewhere. But you couldn't bet on them not being around the yard.'

'Unless someone had called them away. You've got more men than Harry, haven't you?'

'They were over to another farm, this afternoon.'

The two men came back.

'We are agreed we should have Philip here,' Charles said.

'I left a message for him to ring when he
120

came home,' Mamsie said.

'Yes, I know. But we'll have to call the police, you know.'

Lesley interrupted quickly.

'Just a minute. You say you brought her because she wanted to talk to me about a letter. That right?'

'Yes.'

'Then she was in a hurry about it, to come up with you like that?'

'She was. First she said she wanted me to go with her to see you.'

'About this letter?'

'Yes. Then when we got outside your house she changed her mind and I left her there.'

'She didn't come in,' Lesley said. 'She must have waited till you'd gone then come straight here. It was here she wanted to come. The letter was an excuse.'

For a moment Mamsie thought Lesley would start laughing, but the idea passed. Lesley looked calm and innocent again.

'It's not far across the fields,' Eddy said.

'I remember,' Charles said. 'But if all this was as Eddy said, she could not have had an appointment here. So she came for a specific reason, and it was not to call on someone here unannounced.'

'That's for sure,' Eddy said. 'The way across the fields from where she was comes in on the opposite side of the farm from the tithe barn.'

'Then how did she get in there without any of

us seeing?' Mamsie said. 'The only way is to go right round behind the hedge and through the wood to the back of the barn.'

'I thought she didn't know the place?' said Lesley, offhandedly. 'Sounds a bit of a detour for a stranger to succeed in.'

'She might have had a map,' Charles said. 'We must guess because we can't touch anything to make sure if she had one or not.'

'I'm beginning to worry badly about not calling the police,' Mamsie said.

'Supposing,' said Eddy, as if he had not heard, 'this goes back to the rumour about money. Adam's money. That rumour seems to keep cropping up.'

'It seems it wasn't a rumour,' Mamsie said, with some warmth. 'Either he had money himself, or he handled a lot for somebody. Tell them what you told me,' she added, turning to Lesley.

The story of the loan was told just before Philip arrived, so had to be told twice. This put Mamsie's nerves more on edge than ever. It was not so much the frustration at being put off the police call, but the practical inability to do anything at all to clear the fog that had gathered all round her in the last thirty-six hours.

'The money is beginning to appear like a motive,' Philip said. 'Suppose she came here to get it? We can't trace any solicitors who know anything about his affairs, so the name on the letter fragment might mean anything.

'In which case, the name might have been keeping just a direction which someone, appointed by Adam, could follow to find cash. It's got to be cash. Any other sort of money is usually traceable.'

'Okay,' Eddy said. 'So she came to find it, got in pretty secretly—perhaps, as you say, under instruction—to the tithe barn. That suggests money is hidden there.'

'Let's look first,' said Lesley. 'After all, I'm the only one who's seen any of his money,' she added, justifying her immediate interest.

'We must not disturb anything,' Charles said.

'My dear boy,' said Philip, 'no one has phoned the police, so nobody would know whether a search happened before or after the murder, but to satisfy all consciences, Charles as the representative of higher authority, and myself, as an officer of the lower, will make the search together.

'We'll second Harry. He knows most of what's in there. The rest of you, wait here.'

The two went out and fetched Harry from the kitchen, where he had drunk four large cups of tea laced with Millie's dandelion wine so that by then, though unwilling to face anything, he had gained enough confidence to run from it.

'Do I have to?' he said, when asked to help search the barn.

'Harry, you know where everything is,' said Philip. 'That'll be a great help.'

'I don't know where half is,' Harry said. 'When I goes in there for to find something they sends in me meals and a bed.'

Harry, Charles thought, has been swilling.

Philip spoke sharply, then affectionately. Under shock and sedation, Harry thought he might as well go.

He had no chance really of keeping any of the hidden treasure. But he stalled by saying he needed to go to the bog.

Charles and Philip therefore went to the barn on their own.

3

'I believe he knows something,' Charles said, as they entered the great barn. 'He has a furtive look only faintly blushed with booze.'

'You think he has found the money,' Philip said, looking round. 'You could hide elephants in here. We'll wait for him.'

Charles looked thoughtful.

'We are all concealing a crime,' he said. 'I am not sure that it is really doing good.'

'It is simply a delay while we sort out where we are,' Philip said.

'If you ask me, we are all in the vicinity of the soup,' said Charles. 'In order to defend Mamsie from gossip we now find we are supporting her in what may seem to be a charge of two murders.'

'Do you think Adam *was* killed?'

Philip turned to Charles.'

'It would have been easy,' Charles said. 'A narrow road, a drunken man. Mind you, I don't suggest the murderer could have been certain the driver would do what he did eventually do, but he could try and the try came off.'

'That left no evidence,' Philip said. 'This one leaves a chopper with blood on it.'

'If the first death was forced then this one may be a consequence, a necessity. And necessity would have been forced by the first one having been suspected but not proceeded with.'

'And then murder raised by rumour, perhaps organised rumour. But that almost suggests this woman organised the rumour.'

'Well, somebody did,' Charles said, staring up. 'And do you know, if that chopper had been lying up there on one of those great crossbeams and toppled over it would do just what the chopper has done here.'

'Come off it! You've switched from concerted murders to organised Acts of God.'

'Perhaps, but was she hidden there or did she fall down between the bales?' Charles said. 'Suppose she had been climbing the bales— you see they do form very large steps up towards that platform resting on the beams— perhaps the money is hidden up there?'

'Think on your own guesses, Charles. She

walks two miles across the fields and then tries to climb up twenty feet of hay bales. What? In those shoes?'

'I confess it doesn't seem possible to walk far with those slim affairs let alone the stiletto heels, but she is here and we know she was dropped by Eddy the other side of the fields.'

Harry came in and stopped in the doorway as if unwilling to come any further into the barn.

'You're not frightened, Harry,' Philip said. 'What's the matter?'

'Superstitious. It's my mother, she always said—'

'Harry,' said Charles gently, 'I don't think it's superstition. I think it's a guilty conscience.'

'You don't think I did *that*?' Harry bowled.

'Oh no.' Charles shook his head. 'But I think you know where the money is. Now look, man, it can do you no good. Now murder has been done everything in the barn will be turned inside out by the police, and they'll know who did what and if they think you meant to steal money that you found, there'll be trouble for you. You do understand that?'

Harry did not say he did or he didn't, but what he did say would have shocked anyone but a man well protected against such awful things. Even so, Charles raised his eyes to the ceiling, asking that such awful words should be forgiven.

'All right,' Harry said. 'Yes, I know it's no

good. It was just I found it and it was such a lot and I thought nobody wasn't going to notice some gone, that's all.'

'Have you taken any?' said Philip.

'No, I only found it looking for the harness bits and just after—' he swallowed a large gulp of air, '—I found her.'

'Show us where it is,' Charles said.

They went into the little room. Harry shifted stuff he had dragged across so that nobody should notice the trapdoor in the boards.

'What about me fingerprints?' Harry said, straightening.

'Don't worry. You'll tell the police you found this hiding place and the money,' Philip said.

Harry bent again and pulled up the trap. They gathered round looking down into the dark hole to the earth floor.

The earth floor was plainly visible because there was nothing in the hole at all.

CHAPTER NINE

1

Harry spoke a few oaths of surprise so long it became almost a recital until Charles cut him short.

'You put it back here, you say. I suppose the stuff on top of the trapdoor looked as you'd left it? Or do you really remember how you left it, in detail?'

Harry thought a moment, then shook his head.

'I didn't think to look at it like that,' he said.

'And the boxes were quite ordinary?' Philip said.

'Old Eley boxes, used to hold—' he scratched his head, 'I forget how many it was now. We don't get 'em that size not now.'

Charles straightened up from peering down the hole.

'There has been a good deal of traffic through this barn in the last hour,' he said, 'and yet nobody *has* seen anyone go in or out. We must see the secondary doors, probably the one farthest from the house.'

'I'll show you,' Harry said, 'though they don't get used that much when you can just walk in through the big door without opening anything.'

He led the way out of the small room and to the left, passing small heaps of haybales, depleted by the winter feed so that a pair of old wagons could be seen.

'Got to get a wheelwright,' Harry said. 'Need them carts for the new horses when they come.'

The floor was cobbled, hay strewn, and quite useless for showing any traces of people using the side door.

At the end of the barn was a wooden

separating wall for a workshop space, obviously not much used. Beyond that was the side door standing open.

'This is usually shut,' Harry said.

Outside the door was a grassway leading to a field ahead, and on the right a hedge with a gate in it, leading into a wood.

'Dead easy,' Philip said. 'It's a detour from where she started, but it's an easy approach to the barn.'

'Mamsie said the woman had never been here,' Charles said. 'But she knew the way, it seems, just as it seems that the only reason for a secret entry into the barn was the hidden money.'

'Either it was hers or it was meant for her,' Philip said. 'Harry, was Adam Stong ever much in the barn?'

'He used to wander about loose,' said Harry. 'He was always thinking of something or other, he said. Half the time he wouldn't even notice you was there, if you ask me.'

'Thanks, Harry,' Philip said. 'You can finish your tea.'

Harry hesitated.

'Not going to call the cops, then?' he said, uneasily.

'Of course we shall,' Philip said. 'I think Mrs Stong is doing it.'

'I wouldn't have taken that money,' he said. 'Not really. It was just an idea I got when I found it. Such a stinking great lot of it, there was.'

'As far as we know, there never was any money,' said Philip, watching him.

'But oh yes there was,' said Harry. 'There wouldn't be any sense making it up, would there?'

'No.'

Harry looked as if he would say more, then turned and went back round the end wall of the barn towards the house.

'I think the sequence of events was as follows,' Charles said. 'Mrs Marks came here, was met by someone and murdered. Harry, coming to find harness, interrupted the taking of the money by the murderer, but he took it after Harry went out the first time.'

'While Marks was outside talking to Harry?'

'I think so, because he says he came back in here and pretended to tidy up. That's when he found her.'

'So she got Eddy to fetch her up here to get the money. It had suddenly become necessary for her to get it.'

'Apparently when Eddy mentioned Lesley's letter. How did that signal an urgent need to get the money? Did it mean someone else was in the know? But the letter didn't mention any such thing. None of the letters did.'

'Suppose she didn't know about the money at all,' Philip said. 'If she came to see someone because of the letter, who?'

'Eddy must have let her know that Mamsie

130

knew all about them.'

'That leaves Harry and Millie, the two regular hands being at another farm this afternoon.'

'She has casual labour when needed,' Charles said. 'But the hay isn't ready yet, and she didn't mention any extra hands.'

'Well, if she came straight up after alarm at hearing about the letter she couldn't have known anyone would be here at any special time. She didn't phone on the way up and there are no boxes between Lesley's place and here. It's mostly farmland.'

'So she came to see Mamsie,' Charles said firmly. 'I feel sure it was that, but there would be no need to meet Mamsie in a barn, so she met someone on the way.'

'You forget the detour. There would have been no need for that if she came to see Mamsie.'

They went slowly back through the barn to the small room and stopped there, looking to the bale which hid the body of Mrs Marks.

'We have got nowhere,' Charles said. 'We can't hold it up any longer. We shouldn't have done so in the first place.'

'It's going to be difficult for her,' Philip said pointedly. 'If she's accused of this one Adam's going to be thrown in as a bonus.'

'I know. I hoped we might find a way round it, but I don't think there is one.'

'Do you think that whoever killed that

woman also killed Adam by some means that hasn't been found?'

'It does seem to be connected. The trouble with trying to find out the truth in these tragedies is that one finds oneself going over the same things over and over again, hoping one saw it wrong the first time or times. But over and over again there is nothing more to see.'

'There is always something we should have seen,' Philip said.

'You sound more of the cloth than I,' Charles said, and turned to the door. 'We must go back.'

2

'What did you go out after me for?' Harry said, almost in a whisper. 'Eh?'

Millie drew back against the table.

'What's the matter with you, Harry? I felt like a bit of cuddle, that's all.'

'You was supposed to be getting supper ready,' he said.

'I wasn't bothering overmuch. Things is all upside down these days. You knows that. It makes me sort of restless all this coming and going and talking secret. Sometimes I get so I feel he ain't dead after all.' She put her hands to her face for a moment. 'And now she's out there—'

'I thought you knew—the way you come out after me,' he said.

She stood rock still for several seconds, eyes big.

'What do you mean? What do you mean, Harry?'

'Don't bust yourself. I don't mean you did anything, not—I was just talking. Sort of trying to work things out about her.'

'About her? You never seen her before, have you?'

He looked at the kitchen door, then went closer to her.

'Yes. I seen her here.'

'When?'

'Not long back. Forget when, zactly.'

'He was here then?'

'Yes. That is, he wasn't about, but he was alive.'

'What was she doing?'

'She asked me what farm it was. I was over in the wood. Bessie and Janny got out through the hedge on Home Field and in the wood. She was there.'

'What was she doing?'

'She looked she was just walking. She had a map.'

'Why didn't you say you seen her?'

'I wasn't sure. It kept worrying me I thought I'd seen her, then I thought it must be somebody like her. She had black hair then, you see. Black it was, with sort of little grey bits in it.'

'Didn't she say anything? Bout who

133

she was?'

'No she said about cows not having any fun these days—about semination, she was. So I said we haves a bull, and we makes a sort of joke about me being a big feller and that. You know.'

'So what happened?'

'Nothing. She said she fancied me for a bit and she was all right, too, and she said she'd come by the barn gate about nine, but she didn't come.'

'She fancied you,' Millie said, blankly. 'What, a posh woman like her?'

'Them's the worst, sometimes,' he said.

'I suppose you'd know!' she said sharply. 'But you got to tell 'em in there. You know that?'

'Yes. I know that. It's just that I want to have the right time—the right moment.'

'You must know when it was you saw her.'

'It was that hot spell in April. A month—five weeks back. Reckon now she said she'd be there to make sure I was while she went somewhere else.'

'But where would you have been that time, Harry? Nine o'clock! Twas dark then. She was just having you on. But what for? Somebody like her?'

'Don't keep on about somebody like her! What's the matter with me, then?'

'I don't mean that! I mean she must have been trying to stop you going somewhere—'

134

'I know! Twas when I was getting them wagons uncovered in the big barn for when the new horses come.'

Millie looked grim.

'You best go in there and tell 'em now,' she said.

'Twill do when the police is here,' he said.

3

'The phone doesn't work,' Mamsie said.

Philip stared in disbelief. Charles closed the door behind them and looked from Mamsie to Eddy and then to Lesley, who nodded.

'Since when?' Philip said.

'Just now. I got impatient with all this. You try.'

Philip tried. It was quite dead.

'Sinister,' said Eddy, ironically.

'Oh lord, here's another man,' said Lesley staring out of a window. 'You'll have a house full. It's the Marks man. The bereaved husband. Who's going to tell him?'

She almost laughed and looked round at her four companions.

'Let him in, Charles,' Mamsie said. 'We can't keep *him* out.'

Charles let him in.

'These are all my friends,' Mamsie said. 'I'm sorry, but we have just found your wife. She's dead.'

Marks looked at her and then glanced round the other faces.

'How has this happened?' he said at last. 'An accident?'

'It looks like a murder,' said Philip. 'We were just going to ring the police but the phone isn't working.'

'I'm not surprised. The wire's hanging off the pole out there. Cut. One of those long things for snipping bits off trees. It's lying in the road hedge. It made me wonder when I saw it.'

'Don't you want to know what happened, Cully?' said Lesley.

'Are you quite sure she's dead?' said Marks, looking round again.

'She was hit on the head with a small axe,' Philip said. 'She is quite dead.'

He shrugged.

'So that's that,' he said. 'Where is she?'

'She's in the tithe barn,' Charles said. 'I will show you—'

'Oh no, please don't. I don't want to see her. I just want to be sure she's quite dead. She's tried so hard in the past to be killed in one way or another, that I can hardly believe she succeeded at last. There must be dozens of unfortunate suspects with motives. I'm glad you can't call the police. Do you mind if I smoke?'

A car passed in the lane, going slowly.

'Mr Marks feels strongly,' said Lesley. 'And take it from me, he's right. Making enemies was her favourite hobby. She was twisted.'

Eddy looked sharply at her, a line of light

136

shooting in his brain from Lesley, to the letter, to his recognition of the sender, to his visit to her and then to Marks' house and the appearance of the wife. For a moment, it all seemed a very neat network of events, as if somebody had started it and sent it flashing from A to B, on to C and then back to murder.

The door suddenly opened and Mrs Holmes came in from the dusk outside.

'Oh, it's a party,' she said and closed the door behind her.

'It's not,' Mamsie said. 'What do you want?'

'That very nice parson called on me this afternoon,' Mrs Holmes said pointing at Charles. 'I said a bit much and stopped short because I was scared. I think I was wrong.'

'Have you come about Adam?' Charles said. 'We have all been discussing the terrible event. You may speak in front of everyone here.'

'I'm glad of that,' the woman said, suddenly going slack with relief. 'Honestly, I don't think I can keep it to myself much longer.'

'You wouldn't tell me why Adam was drinking so heavily that night,' Charles prompted.

'No. I was frightened really for my husband, but you coming and asking questions sort of tripped my nerves.'

'Sit down,' Mamsie said, offering a chair.

'No. Thanks.' She drew a long breath. 'Well, that night he died he was drinking—insanely. And then all of a sudden he let it out.

'He said somebody was after him. To kill him, and he hadn't the guts to have it out so he might as well get it when he was too drunk to notice anything.'

'He didn't mention any name, of course,' Philip said quietly.

'No. If he had I'd have gone to the police when I heard about the accident, I suppose. But I wasn't sure he didn't mean my husband.'

'Would your husband have threatened him?' Philip said.

'Only to tell him to get out. It wasn't jealousy, if that's what you mean. It was that he wouldn't have Adam round the place at any price. Adam was trouble. I don't think he really meant it. He just couldn't help it. It trailed around with him.'

'Did he lend you any money?' Mamsie said suddenly.

'No.' She laughed. 'He offered to, but I knew the only place he'd get money was from you, so I said if my husband needed any he'd know where to go.'

'Why did he offer it, dear?' said Lesley, almost with sweetness.

'He knew my husband was having troubles. I believed he really wanted to get hold of our property, and a loan is a good way to start.'

'Where is your husband?' said Lesley, sharply.

Mrs Holmes looked at her.

'What's this? A trial?' she said.

'We were thinking it would be nice if everybody who had anything to do with Adam when he died would speak up and kill this rumour about somebody doing it for him.'

The woman looked at her ladyship for a second or more, then turned slightly away.

'I see,' she said.

'There have been a lot of these anonymous letters,' Eddy put in.

'Yes,' she agreed and looked around. 'Have you got any drink in this place? My nerves are quivering.'

'Charles, it's over in the cupboard,' Mamsie said. 'The rest of you, help yourselves.'

Charles crossed the room. The action seemed to break a build-up of tension.

'I don't know where my husband is,' Mrs Holmes said. 'It was one of the things which made me feel bad—so that I had to do something. He went off this morning. He should have been back by four. That's the latest he's ever been on that market. I don't know where he is. He said he would be back, but he hasn't come.'

She stopped suddenly. Charles gave her a drink. It allowed her time to calm down.

'Do you know Mrs Marks?' Lesley said.

Mrs Holmes glanced briefly towards Marks as he stood by the window. Alerted by the question he looked back at her.

'My wife,' he said.

She shook her head. 'I don't think so. To do

with Adam do you mean?' She looked round.

'Why do you think it's to do with Adam?' Philip said gently.

'Well, we were all talking about him—' She hesitated. 'He did say he had a partner. It was when he was trying to push me to take a loan, to show I wouldn't have to deal with him only. He knew I wouldn't do that.'

'I thought you were friends?' Mamsie said.

'What—that little bastard?' she said, not realising who had spoken at once. 'Oh, I'm sorry ... At first I felt sorry for him. I suppose that was his way of getting round people. Then I got the message—'

She broke off, looked at Mamsie and turned away.

Charles went to her.

'What was the message you understood?' he said quietly.

She stood rigidly with her back to the company, and then slowly turned back.

'He was a blackmailer,' she said, hardly opening her teeth. 'Surely I'm not the only one here who knew that?'

CHAPTER TEN

1

There was a silence, not from shock or surprise, but more a pause in which to think what was best to say next.

Mamsie stood looking at Mrs Holmes quietly, almost calculating. Lesley wore a half smile of amusement as she examined her face in her handbag mirror.

Of the four men only Marks looked as if he had heard it all before.

Mrs Holmes turned back and looked from face to face.

'Didn't anybody know?' she said, astonished.

'How did you find out?' Philip said.

'He tried it in a small way. A personal way. He didn't realise my husband and I are very good friends. If I'm worried about something, I ask him what's best to do.'

'Did you tell Jim?' Mamsie said.

'Not at the time. Jim was hot under the collar about Adam. Wouldn't have him anywhere near. I thought Adam might get a beating, and I didn't want that.'

'Did you tell him at any time?' Philip said.

'Yes. After I heard Adam was dead.'

'It does seem that if Adam was frightened someone would kill him, it could not have been Mr Holmes,' said Charles quietly. 'He would hardly have gone to the would-be murderer's house, even drunk.'

Lesley put her mirror away.

'I think it's time we all said what we know,' she said. 'For my part, I knew Adam was blackmailing people because some of them had

141

been to me and complained. It was usually to do with our establishment business. When I found out about it, I didn't have him anywhere near in business hours.

'He and my dead partner were thick as thieves, and I feel quite sure she was in it with him. But I didn't know for certain; it's just my guess.'

'Surely a right guess,' said Eddy. 'It ties the two deaths together and supplies the motive.'

Mrs Holmes sat down abruptly as if too weak to stand any longer. She waved Charles back when he went to help.

'But the money was taken,' said Philip. 'Harry had no way of taking it. He was seen leaving the barn with the harness and going back and he hadn't been there a minute before Millie went in; after that, almost everybody went in.'

'The boxes he described would be about the size of a table cigarette box,' Eddy said, 'and there were about a dozen, he reckons. Taking big notes, which he says they all were, you might get over twenty thousand pounds. Worth taking. But it's a bulky load you'd have. You'd want a sack.'

'There are plenty of old sacks in the barn,' said Mamsie.

'If money was hidden there, and as much as you say,' Marks said, 'then that's what she went for. That's got to be the fact. She knew the money was there and she went to get it. It's possible that someone knew she would go there, sooner or later.'

'That means keeping watch,' said Philip. 'Anyone keeping watch on the barn must have been noticed.'

'Unless it was someone working here,' Marks said. 'Then nobody would have noticed him.'

'I'm not quite clear on the motive which Eddy suggests is there,' Charles said. 'Were the two of them killed because they had together blackmailed some person, or was she blackmailing because she knew Adam had been murdered and why?'

'She knew the murderer,' Eddy said.

'I don't think it'll hold up,' Lesley said. 'I was walking the dog on the downs by the Head when Adam went over. I was coming here about the same time she must have gone into the barn. I could have done both, but there's no motive that applies to me.'

'Not blackmail?' said Charles.

She laughed.

'Me? My dear man! everybody knows what I am. I don't have to pay to keep it quiet.

'So long as it's called Rest, Relaxation, or Recuperation, it's all right, Charles. Besides, how could those two blackmail their own partner in the business?'

'Someone really ought to go for the police,' said Mamsie. 'I'm beginning to feel guilty.'

'You are not alone,' said Charles, almost in a

murmur. 'In guilt feeling, that is.'

'Do you have to fetch the police?' Mrs Holmes said. 'I don't want Jim in trouble. I'm not easy over Adam. Somebody could turn round and say—' She stopped.

'They could say it about anyone,' Eddy said.

It was then that Millie overcame the reluctant Harry and he knocked on the door and came in.

'I think I ought to say I seen her before. She was in the wood last April and I spoke to her and arranged to see her that night, but she didn't turn up. Thanks.'

He turned, and, even as Philip called out, disappeared and slammed the door after him.

Mrs Holmes recovered her voice and began talking again as if she had not noticed Harry's interruption.

'I don't know what did happen that night,' she said quickly, 'but he was talking about being done—and he meant killed. And several times he said it would be better if he did it himself. It would be quicker and he'd know what was going on.

'Before you say anything—he was screwed out of his mind and he rambled, saying things over and over again. Talking to himself. But he did say that.'

'He must have made up his mind to do it before he got to you,' Eddy said. 'That's why he got drunk—so it would be easier—'

He turned towards Lesley.

144

'Did he tell you that?' he said.

All the men seemed to be staring at her.

'I don't remember what he did say. He was off his nut. As she says—rambling. It didn't make any sense. If he did say it, I wouldn't have taken any notice. He hadn't the guts.'

'Why did he call?' Philip said. 'In the state he was in he must have had a reason. He was drunk because he was scared stiff. There was one thing in his mind—to get away from the person he feared, even by suicide. In that state he must have had a reason for going to your house and seeing you?'

Lesley shrugged.

'He said the same to me as to Mrs Holmes. I just left it. He hadn't the guts for suicide. It just wasn't in him. A man who spends a whole lifetime thinking of nobody but himself didn't seem the sort to hurt himself at the end of it.'

'It appeared to him the lesser of two evils,' Charles said.

'Well, he sat down and scribbled a goodbye note,' Lesley said. 'It was just a drunk scrawl. I put my lighter to it and told him to get back home and get some sleep in, then think about it—He just went.'

'If you knew all that, why start the anonymous letters?' Eddy said.

'I should have thought it obvious that I didn't write that letter. My typewriter—yes. My style—almost. It's an easy one to copy. It was popular because clever buggers could

145

imitate it and make fun of it.

'My partner wrote it. The late Mrs Marks.'

'Why did you pretend you did it, Lesley?'

'I thought you'd dismiss it and make no more fuss. I didn't know there were others coming in. My partner must have organised it.'

'So she didn't know he'd talked of killing himself?'

'I suppose not. I didn't think any great importance would be attached to the letter. She was feeling upset and very bitter about his death. I was surprised. I didn't know she had any feelings at all.'

'It wasn't affection she felt,' Marks said. 'It would have been anger. I know.'

'It seems to me,' said Charles, 'that this present revelation gets nowhere at all. He may have thought of suicide, or he may not. The question was, and still is, was he murdered? As the police didn't find out, we're not likely to, but our purpose originally was negative.

'What is it now? There is a murdered woman out there which obviously connects with Adam's death. Therefore who wrote the letter is now of no importance to us. It was hardly likely to be an undetected murderer.'

'But it might be someone who knew him,' Philip said, 'apart from the unfortunate lady in the barn.'

'She might have been killed for the money,' Eddy said. 'Meant to knock her out, hit too hard and that was that.'

146

'I think it more likely she was killed by the man Adam was running from that night,' Philip said. 'And as we now know Adam was a blackmailer, there must have been several people who might have done this.'

'You all talk about this as if it were someone right outside and away from here,' said Mamsie, after a watchful silence. 'It's more likely to be someone near, or even here.'

There was a short silence, then Marks spoke directly to Mamsie.

'I noticed, Mrs Stong, that you were not surprised when this lady told us your husband had been a blackmailer. You'd known that?'

'Yes.'

'Had you known it long?'

'Not very long.'

'Just before he died?'

'Yes.'

'Did you speak with him about it?'

'No.'

'Surely it was very important?'

'I heard on the morning he took the pick-up in for service. I never saw him after that.'

'You heard after he'd gone?' said Charles. 'And you had no other vehicle here that day?'

'No.'

'Then you heard the sorry news on this farm?' Charles said.

'Yes. Eddy, will you fetch the police? We cannot go on any longer just talking about things like this.'

'But just a moment, Mamsie,' Philip said. 'One of your staff was involved. That's what you mean, isn't it?'

'Go for the police, Eddy!' Mamsie almost shouted.

There was a knock at the door, which opened almost at the same time. The gravedigger and poet looked in.

'Sam,' said Charles.

'Oh, it's a party,' said Sam, coming into the room. He looked askance at Mamsie as he closed the door. 'A surprise.'

'Quite,' said Philip.

He noticed that Mamsie seemed almost relieved to see the newcomer.

2

'Why did you come out to me in the barn?' Harry said.

Millie looked at the night out of the window.

'Like I said. I got all lonely and frightened and wanted a cuddle.'

He came closer and spoke low.

'Mill, I reckon you was in the barn when I found that money, and I reckon you couldn't go out of it without being spotted, so you pretended you'd come out to find me.'

'How can you think that? It's awful to think that!'

'Otherwise you'd have thought I'd gone home, or on me way. The van was outside. I only went back in to get rid of him out there. I

148

reckon you was in the barn all the time, Mill.'

'You was going to steal it, Harry. I know.'

'So you thought you'd best have it than me?' He looked puzzled.

'I'd look after it better, Harry. It's long past time we were wed.'

'I would have wed you sooner. But he took all me money. You know that? Sometimes he seemed to forget and then he'd come up smiling and remind me—I'm glad he's dead—'

He stopped, his face went white.

'Mill—you was in the barn when she came tonight?' He whispered, his eyes wide, searching her face.

'Yes. I thought she'd come for you. I went to shove her out, and she tripped over the wagon shaft—those old wagons you uncovered—the tyre's half off that wheel, that iron tyre, sticking out where it come off—'

'You didn't hit her?'

'No. She fell on the wheel. The tyre cut her head so bad she didn't even cry. I pulled her behind the bales and scattered the loose straw bits over the floor there.

'It was only half done when you came in. I was going to tell you then, but I was too scared, Harry. I couldn't have told, so I just stood and I saw you with all that money on the table—it seemed like a way out—

'I was all to bits. I wasn't thinking straight. When you went out I took the boxes and put them back of the wagons. Then I saw you come back again and—

'Well, I really did need a cuddle then—I saw you find her—

'I went all cold, Harry. It just wasn't me any more. You said what's the matter with me, and I sort of froze and pretended I didn't know anything about her. I didn't know meself. I don't know when I think how I said those things—' She broke off finally and she looked at him with tears running down her cheeks.

'You saw me with her before, when she came, April,' he said slowly.

'I was coming back from chickens. I heard over the hedge. I watched that night but she didn't come. I didn't think she ever would.'

He walked to the table and back again and stopped.

'We'll have to tell Missus,' he said, and looked at her, then took her in his arms. 'Oh, Mill, Mill. Why did you go and hide her like that? It makes folk think—Oh, Mill—'

'Twas all I could think of. I felt I'd done it meself. Specially when I shoved her—you see, I would have pulled her hair off, I would. I thought she was coming for you—Harry—'

'I reckon she was coming for that money. You didn't think it was mine, did you, Mill?'

'Well, of course I did. As you never had any money I thought you'd been saving it secret, for a surprise. It was just a joke—it seemed like it then, I mean.'

'But there was thousands—hundreds of

thousands!'

'I only saw you lift out one box. I didn't think like that. About a lot of money. I was a bit ashamed first, spying like and went away down the barn, and then I got mad thinking you were keeping it secret and always pretending you didn't have none—' She shook her head. 'It was all a mess inside me head, one thing after another like it did—'

'Look. I'll get missus out here. You tell her. She'll know what to do, Mill. Don't worry.'

3

'May I take a practical line?' said Marks. 'I knew my wife had been indulging in crime of some sort, and when I heard of Adam's death, I thought she had something to do with it. They were always together in schemes to trick people out of money.

'While here I discovered that she intended to go away, disappear. This suggested to me that she had enough money to do it now that Adam was dead. I thought it would be good for everybody if she did go.

'It would also ease my mind from suspicion that she killed him by some means.

'Fate has saved us any further trouble on her behalf. She is dead. She will be thought to have gone away for good. We have here an itinerant gravedigger and a parson. Why not dig a grave and bury the dead with due ceremony where I understand the new stable floor will be covered in cement this week? She hated horses.'

The effrontery of the suggestion created a pause because the listeners could feel a weird sincerity behind it.

'You can't be serious!' Philip said.

'He's perfectly serious,' said Eddy, almost admiringly.

Charles raised his eyebrows and looked with regret at the floor.

'I can't think of a more succinct manner of putting the whole thing into perspective,' said Lesley, smiling.

Mrs Holmes said nothing but looked from one face to another, speculating on the value of hope.

Sam looked up from rolling a cigarette.

'I am perfectly capable of digging square holes in any situation except granite,' he said.

There was another silence, thoughtful this time.

'We cannot seriously—' Philip began, when there was a knock and the door opened.

Harry looked in. 'Missus, please would you come and see Millie? I think she's a bit off.' He stood staring at Mamsie as if trying to hypnotise her into coming without question.

Mamsie went.

'Well,' Lesley said, 'I have cast my vote in favour. I've done nothing, so I think I shall go.'

'We shall need mourners,' said Marks.

Lesley stopped and looked at him.

'I believe you knocked her off,' she said.

She noticed Mrs Holmes sitting on the chair with her eyes shut.

'I wish it could—just stop,' Mrs Holmes said in a near whisper. 'I wish it could.'

'So does everybody else,' Lesley said. 'We've been here all the bloody evening and now and again somebody says, "We must call the police!" hoping that nobody will. Or just shifting the conscience load on to everybody else. And do you know what?' She looked round. 'Nobody complained. They looked serious, responsible, took it on and then unloaded it again on everybody else.

'To me it seems everybody made their minds up, to start with, to handle this by their little selves. Now that does seem responsible to me.'

'I can't be party to any such action,' said Philip.

'Well, go home and forget it,' Lesley said. 'I vote for that because it is the kindest for people left. She meant to leave us. That would have been fine. She has left us, but can't come back. That's finer.'

'It's sometimes difficult to see the way of law,' said Eddy. 'As has been said, we have all the necessary equipment for the job. Done tonight, finished.

'Call the police. All sorts of innocent people dragged in over the hope that one in a dozen will be the murderer. Inquests. Trials. Everybody hauled in, sent away, hauled in, bitched, bothered, bewildered for months—'

Mamsie came back.

'It was an accident,' she said. 'She fell and hit her head on the cart wheel. Milly saw it, but she was so upset she's been sort of numbed.'

'Then any objection to fetching the police is—' Philip began.

Marks cut in.

'We have behaved with great responsibility,' he said.

'We are the people concerned with the death of Mrs Marks—'

'God rest her soul,' murmured Charles.

'Then let us deal with the matter in a responsible and civilised manner,' Marks went on. 'Let us take a vote.'

'This will land everybody in prison,' said Philip quietly.

'If it does,' said Sam, lighting a malformed cigarette, 'you'll be responsible. Are we agreed to that? Good. He always was a prissy beggar. What was it about courage that Voltaire wrote?'

Philip looked round. 'Mark me as an abstainer,' he said.

The concrete was poured next afternoon. Charles came to have a farewell tea with Mamsie.

'Do you always keep that gun in the corner, dear?' he said.

'It's the customary place. One umbrella, one gun.'

'I think you supported Lady Lesley once?'

'It was only a small thing.'

'Fancy her walking her dog almost in the very place of the passing of Adam.'

'A fine place for air after a long day. I like it up there.'

'You were always a walker of note. Faster than we were, I remember. I do love cream.' He put more cream on the jam on the butter on his bap and bit with slow pleasure. 'Why did you rush off to town with that epitaph, Mamsie?'

'I had a feeling that things might happen because Adam and she were always together in things. I thought my friends would be a help.'

'Wasn't it a roundabout way to get help?'

'I don't know. The way I did it I didn't ask for anything, you see. They came to me. I needed them because I'd found out that Harry was one of Adam's—victims. I wanted protection for my people.'

'You had it. But I never saw the real epitaph; the one you asked Jamey to do on the stone.'

She laughed and got up. She went to her desk and brought back her writing on the seed merchants' order form.

Charles read:

Here lies Adam Stong.
Lecher.
Am I glad God's got him?
Betcher.

155

He looked at her.

'Mamsie,' he said reprovingly, 'I'm ashamed of you! Such English!'

We hope you have enjoyed this Large Print book. Other Chivers Press or G.K. Hall & Co. Large Print books are available at your library or directly from the publishers.

For more information about current and forthcoming titles, please call or write, without obligation, to:

Chivers Press Limited
Windsor Bridge Road
Bath BA2 3AX
England
Tel. (01225) 335336

OR

G.K. Hall & Co.
P.O. Box 159
Thorndike, Maine 04986
USA
Tel. (800) 223–2336

All our Large Print titles are designed for easy reading, and all our books are made to last.